EDWINA PARKHURST, SPINSTER

EDWINA PARKHURST, SPINSTER

Patricia Lucas White

Five Star
Unity, Maine

Five Star First Edition Romance Series.
Published in 2000 in conjunction with Patricia Lucas White.

Cover photograph by Jillian Raven.

Set in 11 pt. Plantin by Rick Gundberg.

Printed in the United States on permanent paper.

Library of Congress Cataloging-in-Publication Data

White, Patricia Lucas, 1941–
    Edwina Parkhurst, spinster / by Patricia Lucas White.
      p.   cm. — (Five Star first edition romance series)
    ISBN 0-7862-2584-X (hc : alk. paper)
    1. Women novelists — Fiction. 2. Kidnapping — Fiction.
3. Oregon — Fiction. I. Title. II. Series.
    PS3573.H47459 E39   2000
    813′.6—dc21   00-039403

EDWINA PARKHURST, SPINSTER

Chapter One

Outskirts of St. Louis, August 1877

"Miss Edwina? You in there?"

It was a silly question. Where else could she be? The attic was stifling hot, making Edwina Parkhurst glow far more than was seemly for a lady. The cluttered, unfinished attic, with its small enclosed space she had fashioned for the battered rolltop desk and single wooden chair, was the only completely private and lockable room in the old, over-crowded house. And given her morally unacceptable occupation, privacy was as essential as deceit.

Even if it was an unwelcome interruption, Edwina knew Martha Biggs who was, after years of service, more family than family retainer wouldn't have climbed the steep stairs without ample reason. She was prepared to hear nothing good when the old woman rapped on the door again.

"You best hurry, child," Martha said. "They be trouble." Without waiting for Edwina's reply, and with scant respect in her voice, she added, "Lord have mercy on us all, that no-gumption sister of yours be a fool for listening to a man like that. A pure-dee simpleton, if you was to be asking. But you ain't, and I ain't having no truck with any of this, no matter what your ma says contrary."

Martha's retreat, the stair creaking under her heavy tread, took away any need Edwina Parkhurst had to defend her

7

older sister's mental capacity, but it didn't take away the fact that there was trouble. In this house trouble always called Edwina's name—and expected an immediate answer. Sighing, she cleaned the steel nib of her pen with the flannel wiper, returned them both to her writing case, capped the ink bottle, closed and locked the desk. Using the tail of her all-enveloping apron she mopped her face, but it was no use trying to tidy her hanging braid of chestnut hair—nor any real reason to do so.

The family was used to seeing her inky-handed, with possibly a smear or two elsewhere on her person, and there was no one else who mattered. This was a house full of women, three generations of women, all of them her responsibility.

Even the stuffy air in the narrow stairwell felt cool after the heat of the attic, but Edwina didn't linger. Lifting her skirts and starched petticoats, she hurried down to do battle with whatever constituted their latest trouble. It was waiting in the form of her older sister in the front parlor.

"The preacher said I have to . . ." Olivia's voice broke. She tried unsuccessfully to swallow back a sob. Finally, she just stood in the middle of the room, bonnet dangling from her fingertips, auburn hair straggling loose, tears running down her pale face.

Halting in the doorway between the front and back parlors and taking a deep breath, Edwina forced her voice into tones of deceptive gentleness. "Have to what, Livy?"

Her sister dropped the black velvet bonnet, put both gloved hands to her face and rocked back and forth, sobbing.

The moaning and the tears weren't unusual. As their mother's sister, Auntie Jean, was wont to say with pursed lips and a shake of her head, "Livy is afraid of her own shadow and can weep to prove it." She usually added, "All because of that horrid man. Poor soul. Poor, dear soul."

Pity was way down on the list of emotions Edwina was feeling. But, if she wanted to get any more work done this day, she had to calm her sister. Edwina looked around the crowded room, locating the vial of smelling salts before she wended her way through the maze of small, well-draped tables, curio cabinets, and hassocks, all with their burden of fringe, tassels, figurines, keepsakes, portraits, oddities, and other dust catchers. Smelling salts in hand, Edwina walked across the deep red carpet, halting before her black-clad sister who still wept uncontrollably.

"Livy," Edwina said, "it can't be that bad. Just tell me and we can . . ."

"My Christian duty . . ." Livy sobbed. "Have to go . . . The preacher said I . . . burn in hell if I don't . . . submit . . ."

With his hellfire-and-damnation sermons and sly, lecherous eyes, Preacher Halbert wasn't one of Edwina's favorite people. Barely managing to suppress a snort of derision, Edwina noticed the girls, Livy's two daughters Meg and Becca, and her own black-gowned mother, standing in the shadows of the entry hall. They looked scared and helpless, but as much as she loved the three of them, their fear would have to wait. She put her hand on Livy's arm, gave it a shake, perhaps a little more vehemently than she intended, and demanded, "Tell me!"

"Ambrose."

"What about him?" Edwina's mouth tightened, but she managed to keep her voice neutral. She was hoping her sister had finally decided on a divorce. But she knew, given the tenets of the preacher's church and her sister's pious nature, that a divorce for any reason was only wishful thinking.

Behind her she heard the rocking chair squeak as Auntie Jean laid aside her fancy sewing and got to her feet—and she also heard her aunt's exclamation of dismay at the mention of

Livy's husband's name. Ambrose Raiter wasn't an acceptable topic of conversation in Edwina's house and hadn't been in the last six years. The beast had taken off for points west without a word and left his wife and daughters destitute and dependent on Edwina, the woman he had hatefully called a vinegar-tongued old maid.

There was no immediate answer from Olivia, unless a near-swoon, a sniff of salts, being helped by Edwina and Jean to the medallion-back settee, could be considered her response. She reclined there as others fussed over her, tucking pillows under her head, loosening her garments, fanning her with the ostrich feather fan, and offering her a sip of brandy.

The grandfather clock in the entry had bonged the half-hour before Edwina got her answer. It came from her younger niece, Becca, and not from Livy, who had consented to take a draught of Dr. Miscker's sleeping powders and to being led up the stairs to her bed by her mother and older daughter.

"Papa wrote a long letter. Mama got it this afternoon and went straight to talk to the preacher. He said she had to go, that it was her wifely duty to submit to her husband's will and obey him in all things." The words came out in the barest of whispers, and Becca, nearing thirteen and something of a beauty, caught her trembling lower lip in her teeth. "We have to go, too, and I don't . . . Aunt Wina, I'm afraid. He'll hurt her again, I know he will. And maybe us, too."

Holding her fury in check, Edwina patted her niece's hand as she asked, "Go where? Where is he?"

"Oregon."

"Oregon?"

"He said he had a homestead there in the southeastern part. We are supposed to take the train to a place in Nevada, Winnemucca I think, and then go from there two hundred miles across the wilderness in a wagon." The girl flung herself into Edwina's arms, clutched her with frantic hands, and wailed, "You have to come with us. Mama's not strong enough to go all the way out there alone."

The child soothed and put off with generalities, Edwina returned to the parlor, not the attic, to pace, not write—even though the deadline for the promised work was looming. Auntie Jean's needle flashed in and out of her embroidery. Somewhere in the distance a dog barked. Nearby the clock ticked away the minutes, growing louder and louder, or so it seemed, intruding on her worries, reminding her of Livy's tears of despair. "She doesn't have to go, Auntie."

"Yes, dear, she does. Even as a maiden lady, you know that as well as I do. Ambrose is her husband in the eyes of the State and the Lord. It is her bounden duty to do as he says, to be meek and obedient in all ways."

Biting back a sharp and unseemly retort, Edwina asked, "Even if she dies of fear, or worse? The man's a fiend."

Jean dropped the needlework to her lap and looked at Edwina. "Dear, I know you believe yourself to be a free-thinker, but our Livy is a moral, God-fearing woman, just like her dear mother. If she sees this as her lot in life, she will accept it as most wives do."

"She's a fool, and you know it."

"Nonsense! I know nothing of the kind."

Whirling around, Edwina stomped out of the room and into the kitchen, kicking her skirts aside with every angry step, hoping to find some lemonade in the icebox. Martha forestalled her with a quick question, "You be going with her?"

"I don't know. There's money in the bank to keep us a year or longer, but I've committed to deadlines and . . ." She turned away from Martha's knowing eyes and went to the back door, looking at but not seeing the backyard, the path that led to the privy, the sheets hanging limp on the clothes-line.

Coming up to stand behind her, bringing with her the odor of lye soap, camphor, and horehound drops, Martha put her hands on Edwina's shoulders. "Best take warning, child. That preacher's been yelling about evil in them dime novels for the past year or more. And every time he be looking in your direction. I'm thinking he knows about you."

Still worrying about Olivia, but not entirely removed from her imaginary world of handsome gunfighters, murderous Indians, damsels in distress, and other bits of melodramatic derring-do, Edwina felt a twinge of guilty shame. But her voice was flat as she answered, "When Preacher Halbert puts money in my pockets and food on our table, then I'll trying writing something more to his moral taste."

"It's hard on you, child, keeping secrets, letting everyone think all you write is sweet little pieces for *Godey's Lady's Book* and *Capper's Weekly*. You're doing what needs be to keep 'em eating and covered decent."

She patted Edwina's shoulder before she added, "You'll be going with Livy, and paying for the whole trip, your ma'll see to that 'cause it ain't proper for Livy and the girls to travel alone. It'll be up to you, like always."

"No, I . . ." Knowing Martha was right, that that was exactly what her mother would expect, Edwina stopped in mid-protest—knowing, too, that she would do whatever her mother wanted, would do almost anything to spare her any more pain.

Almost as if she could read Edwina's thoughts, Martha's hands tightened for just a second and her voice held a hint of kindness when she murmured, "Go do your scribbling, child, and leave me be. Like as not, you'll have a lot to do afore you be leaving."

Nodding agreement, Edwina gnawed on her lower lip and left Martha stirring the beans that were simmering in a black iron pot on the big wood-burning cookstove.

The rose-shaded coal oil lamp was lit and adding its own acrid heat to the attic before Edwina penned the final page of Lobo Chance's latest dime novel, *Young Nell: or Lost Among the Savages*. Satisfied but weary and alone, Edwina sat for a long time contemplating her immediate future. Eventually she stood, straightened her back and went down the stair, ready to smile and nod agreement when her mother said, "Olivia isn't strong like you, dear. We can't let her go out into that heathenish land all alone. Aunt Jean and I are not well enough to accompany her. You must go to take care of her and the girls."

After all, that's what old maids are for, wasn't it? Edwina thought wryly, swallowing back the lump that was forming in her throat. She was sure, despite the low regard afforded those of her status, that being an independent woman was far more to her liking than being married to a beast like Ambrose Raiter. With that sureness came a small, cherished memory of a long ago kiss in the moonlight, whispered vows of eternal love, and a tearful farewell to a young man in uniform. He was, according to her father and mother, most unsuitable.

"Perhaps he was," she whispered, but there was no real way of ever knowing; a war had seen to that. Nonetheless, her lips were soft with remembering when she went down to join her widowed mother.

Chapter Two

Northwestern Nevada, early November, 1877

Easing sideways in the saddle in an attempt to relieve a body wearied and cramped from traveling too far and too fast, Talmadge Jones reined in his gray gelding just below the top of a small rise. He narrowed his eyes and peered off into the far distance. The dust was still there, hanging in the air for a long time before it did a little dancing and flirting with the wind, then drifting away, fading back into the grayish monotone of the high desert landscape of alkali, sage, and rabbit grass.

The way Tal saw it, that dust coming from the wheels of a train of freight wagons, wasn't getting any closer. It seemed to be angling off toward the west, away from the direction it was supposed to be traveling. That caused him some worry. He couldn't figure the why of it, not when the wagons were supposed to be, according to the man who had hired him, moving straight toward where Tal was sitting atop his gelding.

Four days' worth of whiskers darkened his face and added a little length to his handlebar mustache. The dark, silver-threaded beard had caught itself a crop of dust and grime. He gave his jaw an absent scratch as he pondered the vast expanse of sage and sand, and the dust trail of what he hoped was his quarry: the five wagons of drinking liquor he had been hired to guard. A man had to be cautious, especially with some of the Bannocks and Paiutes off the reservation and doing a little burning, killing, and marauding.

The Indians weren't the big worry, though. It was something else, something he had heard and didn't want to believe, yet it kept nagging at him. Ambrose Raiter, the saloon owner who had hired him, wasn't an easy man, and he had made himself a few enemies.

Tal scratched at his whiskers again. Raiter's wife was supposed to be traveling to Oregon from Winnemucca. If she had any sense at all, Mrs. Raiter would likely wait until late spring before she tried crossing the two hundred miles of uninhabited Nevada high desert separating the railroad station in Winnemucca from Raiter's place in southeast Oregon. Late fall and winter was a bad time for traveling across the long stretch of rocks, sand, and sage with only a few wind-swept wagon tracks for a guide.

Still, even if he hadn't mentioned his wife, it was strange that Raiter had hired Tal to meet the wagon train at Sod House, near the Nevada-Oregon state line, to protect the liquor and not in Winnemucca, the beginning of the journey.

Whatever he thought, it didn't do much for the present, or change the itchy feeling he was having about his employer. Brutal to beasts and women, the saloon owner might be up and coming in the Oregon cow country, but he wasn't much of a man to Tal's way of seeing. He had heard that Raiter needed the presence of his wife to quiet the speculation of the respectable citizens who were against his political ambitions. Still with only three silver cartwheels, a gold double eagle, and a couple of half-dimes—about twenty-three dollars and change—standing between him and what was shaping up to be a long cold winter, Tal didn't much care who was hiring his guns. No matter what else they said about him, Tal always gave a man what he paid for, and usually with little difficulty—not many troublemakers were eager to tangle with Talmadge Jones.

Other than that pack of damn fool muleskinners down there sloping off in the wrong direction, this time didn't look to be much different. Or maybe it did. Something wasn't right. He hadn't lived by the gun this long by ignoring his feelings, and they were doing their damnedest to tell him bad trouble was on the way.

Narrowing his eyes, Tal looked west and peered at the barest trail of dust that rose against a growing wall of dark clouds. Weather breeders, by the looks of them, carrying blow and snow in their bellies and coming in slow and ponderous, like they were fixing to set and stay a spell. By his reckoning, the storm wouldn't be close before late the next day.

Taking off his sweat-stained black Stetson, Tal whacked it against his knee, giving a little grunt of satisfaction at the result, and then creased it carefully before he returned it to his head. He dug a strip of jerky from his vest pocket, and said, "Let's get for getting, horse. We've got us some moving to do if we want to save Raiter his drinking liquor and get us enough money to winter someplace warm."

It couldn't be lost.

There wasn't room in the fancy, yellow-wheeled two-seater to lose a flea. It had to be in there. But it wasn't, that much she could see.

Tired and irritated, Edwina backed out of the buggy, jumped to the ground and stood for a moment trying to think where she could have put the japanned writing box with its new tale of misdeeds and high adventure in the Wild West. It was a tale she had started in the hotel in Winnemucca, and regardless of fatigue, had worked on every evening of their five-day journey across the high desert.

Tapping the toe of her dusty Balmoral boot on the ground, hands on her hips, she stood behind the buggy looking absently at the camp. Six freight wagons, including the one that held their scanty belongings and a few supplies Ambrose had ordered Livy to bring, were standing in a halfcircle; mules being fed and watered, including the two, Big Red and Rude, that she had unhooked from the buggy earlier and led over to the picket line; a campfire where one of the muleskinners was heating something in an iron pot hung on a tripod over the flames; the rest of the skinners making ready for the night.

"Aunt Edwina."

The whisper came from the other side of the wagon just in front of her. She stepped around the vehicle to confront her niece. "Meg? Why on earth are you hiding?"

"I didn't want Mama to see me."

Her face was hidden within the shadows of her sunbonnet, but judging from the sniffing and the quaver in her voice, Edwina was sure the girl was crying. Moving closer, Edwina asked, "Why? What's the matter?"

"Mama . . ."

Certain she had been found out, that her dreadful deeds had come to light, Edwina's hands clenched and she could feel a vein throbbing in her temple, but she only said, "Olivia opened my box and found my writing? Is that what you're trying to tell me?"

Meg nodded. "It was my fault. I just wanted some paper to write to Grandma. Please," she whispered, "don't be mad at Mama. She was crying. Oh, Aunt Edwina, she loves you, but the preacher said those terrible books were leading young men straight to Hades."

"I know what that idiot preacher said," Edwina snapped,

17

letting anger overwhelm the shame. Whirling away from her niece in a swirl of skirts and petticoats, she stomped, with little puffs of whitish dust rising with every furious step, across to where her sister stood near the wooden water barrel mounted on the side of the lead wagon.

Hands clasped before her, black shawl pulled tight around her shoulders, Olivia was looking at Edwina with an expression of deep sorrow. "Oh, Edwina, you were raised to be good and pure. How could you sink to such depths of depravity and shame us so? Mother and Auntie will never be able to lift their heads again."

It was high melodrama, worthy of some of her less respectable literary efforts, but the basic unfairness wasn't easy to bear. Nonetheless, Edwina didn't say, "My shameful secret has kept our whole family fed, clothed, and out of the poorhouse, you and your daughters included." But she did say, chin high, eyes blazing, "Why? Because I didn't think I could support all of us with the pittance I would earn as a woman of easy virtue."

Her fingers rushed to cover her mouth and Olivia gasped.

One of the muleskinners snickered.

Edwina didn't care. Instead, she licked the bitter dust from her dry lips and glared. "Where is it? What did you do with it?"

"Edwina, sister, don't. I beg of you, if you won't think of yourself, think what your sinful ways are doing to those of us who love you."

"Where?"

Olivia took a step back and pressed herself against the side of the wagon, looking for all the world as if she expected Edwina to attack her with pitchforks, horns, and fire, Satan's tools. Meg ran between them, spreading her arms protectively before her mother.

For one unforgivable moment, Edwina was sorely tempted to grab both sister and niece and shake some sense into their silly heads. Instead she sighed, moderated her tone, and asked, once again, "Where did you dispose of my writing case, Olivia? Even if you don't approve of my behavior, that box is mine, and I want it. Where did you put it, Olivia?"

Timid in most things, but unexpectedly stubborn in this, Livy shook her head, sending up a small cloud of dust from her black bonnet. She was saved from answering by the cook's shout, "Come and get it, or I'll throw it out!"

Her arm around her daughter's shoulders, Olivia started to move away from the wagon, pausing beside Edwina long enough to say with moral righteousness, "My dear sister, don't you know I would rather have starved to death than grown rich on the wages of your sins? That I would rather die than know that I am the cause of your damnation? Mama and Auntie will feel the same way, and it breaks my heart that I must write and tell them and our dear preacher of this. It pains me beyond your knowing that I must cause them the sorrow that you have caused me. But I must for I cannot condone evil by my silence."

Hurt by her sister's condemnation and pious ingratitude, Edwina said not a word. Anger gripped her throat, but pride kept her erect and love for her family, if not for her sister at that moment, kept her silent.

Touching her eyes with a scrap of linen and lace, head bowed, Olivia walked slowly over to the campfire where their dinner and Becca were waiting with a group of muleskinners who were pretending to be interested in everything except the drama between Edwina and her sister. Olivia wasn't too upset to accept the tin plate of food that Becca handed her, but Edwina's appetite was gone.

The orange sun, looking impossibly large, was sliding

down behind a massive pile of purplish clouds on the western horizon, but it wasn't yet dark. The wind swirled around, kicked up a twist of dust and flung it into the smell of venison stew then hit Edwina full in the face, almost choking her. Wiping her face, stumbling a little on the uneven ground, she went to the water barrel and used the tin dipper. She had just taken a sip when one of the skinners, a bandy-legged, balding oldster with only three teeth left in his mouth, eased over to where she was standing. Shorty, as he had insisted she call him, had taught her how to drive the mules that pulled the fancy buggy and answered every question she asked. Much to Olivia's disapproval of the familiarity, he called Edwina by her first name when he wasn't taking advantage of his years and calling her "child."

He stood there a moment before pushing back his hat with two fingers, clearing his throat. "Edwina, I ain't one for coming between kin, but I reckon she's wronging you. Your sister took that box of yourn, looked inside it, and liked to swooned on the spot. Then she took her a hike over to the lip of that gully and pitched the whole shooting match over the edge."

"Thank you for telling me, Shorty," Edwina said and walked away, heading in the direction he had indicated, knowing it was useless, that nothing of the writing remained. The wind was as ruthless as her sister, and between them they would have destroyed what had taken Edwina many weary hours of labor to produce.

Shivering in the cold, she wasn't aware the old mule-skinner was walking beside her until he said, "Child, I'd be mighty pleased iffen you'd . . ." He shrugged out of his heavy wool coat and draped it over her shoulders as he added, lowering his voice so only she could hear, "Go along now and do what you hafta do. I'll see to it that there ain't a soul comes a-bothering you."

The coat smelled of sweat and mule and dirt, but Edwina was grateful for its warmth and for his concern. She thanked him as she put her arms into the garment and buttoned it snug.

He stood there a moment longer. "I ain't knowing the straight of it, but there's something going on that stinks to high heaven. Raiter be your kin, too, and I ain't got the right to bad-mouth him, but there's been a heap of whispering going on about his wife and the girls and maybe even you, and I've got me a notion that . . . Oh, don't pay me no mind. Just go on down and get what's yourn. But be careful, child. Real careful. My old bones are telling me something bad's gonna happen." That said, Shorty turned and strode away without giving her any more advice.

She knew in a vague way that he was trying to warn her but Edwina's attention was on the deep gully and its burden of white, wind-blown papers hidden in the deepening shadows. Slipping and sliding down the steep, rocky canyon wall, she made her own cloud of dust before she reached the bottom. A final gift from her father, the sturdy case had withstood the rigors better than she expected and could probably be repaired. The ink bottle was shattered. She found two of the steel nibs and one holder, but all else was lost, broken, or scattered. There was another writing box and more supplies in her trunk, but her writing wasn't as easily replaced.

Standing in the bottom of a deep ravine, the sky growing perceptively darker, Edwina Parkhurst felt more desolate than she had ever felt in her life.

Reaching down she picked up a piece of paper, looked at what remained of the torn sheet and stumbled down the narrow gorge, picking up papers Livy had thrown to the wind and desert.

Edwina retreated far down the canyon. She crept into the

shadows, finally hiding herself in a deep crevasse that had been water-gouged into the back of a huge rock. The wind rose to new heights, howling down the ravine as she huddled in her meager shelter.

The moon was already up and far to the west when a burst of sound, sharp and cracking, slammed into her consciousness, jerking her into a dry-mouthed, fearful awareness. Disoriented, Edwina sat up, looked around, saw nothing beyond the darkness of pooled moon shadows and light-glittered frost on the patches between.

She strained her ears as a blast of sound and a barrage of explosive noise assaulted her.

"Olivia!" She flung the hoarse, anguished cry into the night sky and started to run, retracing the path she had taken earlier. She prayed with every labored breath that her sister and nieces were safe, that the gunfire wasn't coming from their camp, that the muleskinners weren't trying to repel a superior force of attacking Paiutes and Bannocks intent on pillage and murder.

She knew, with a terrible certainty, that it was Indians. She stumbled, fell full-length, knocking the breath from her lungs and scratching the side of her face on a rock.

Talmadge Jones spurred the gelding to greater effort, swore at himself as the animal stumbled and almost fell in the shadowed moonlight. "Easy, boy," Tal said, reining in a little, letting the horse pick his way down the ruts that the mule train had left, marking its passage.

The second outbreak of gunfire was close enough for him to rein the sweating horse to a stop, swing down, and pull the Winchester from the saddle boot. He levered a shell into the chamber and made his cautious way across the bleached-bone white of an alkali playa and up a small rise.

The freight wagons were just beyond—the wagons and whoever was doing the shooting. Slipping from shadow to shadow, he crouched, ran, paused to listen, then ran again until he was at the back of the end wagon. He waited, trying to separate friend from foe, if that's the way the game had to be played. It wasn't long before Tal got his first shock.

"Please! Please, for the love of God, I beg you, don't hurt my girls! They're only babies!" The words were soft, filled with despair, and female.

A woman? Out here? With her babies? Riding with Raiter's drinking liquor and a pack of brainless skinners? It didn't make a lick of sense, but it had to be Raiter's wife.

What was going on? Those two questions gave Tal a flicker of disquiet. He lowered his guard for a fraction of a second.

Just as he heard the woman cry, "Help me. Oh, Ed . . ." The sound was cut off in mid-word by a triggered six-gun. The hot lead found its target. Blood streaming down his face, Talmadge Jones, gunfighter, dropped where he stood, sprawled on the cold sand at the rear of a freight wagon with his Colts still holstered and his Winchester unfired.

Chapter Three

The sound of male voices froze Edwina in place. The words distorted, unintelligible, came from above and to her right. She was sure she was the object of the unseen men's search. And she was equally sure she didn't intend to be found.

"Indians," she said, mouthing the word.

Moving slowly, scarcely daring to breathe, she gathered her bulky skirts and Shorty's heavy coat close around her and crept into the moon shadows at the base of the wall. She huddled there hoping she was nothing more to the searchers than a darkness within other darknesses, not a woman scared almost out of her wits.

Edwina stifled a cry when a shower of rocks clattered down from the rim, starting small landslides of dust and alkali that poured onto her bonnet and bent shoulders. She put her fist in her mouth to keep back a moan of terror when voices shouted orders. Edwina crouched closer to the wall and tried to pray when guns fired, the sound deadly and without mercy.

The moon disappeared behind a fast-moving cloud and reappeared, shaping the concealing shadows into new configurations. Her body cramped and aching, Edwina crept with the shadows, slithered in between two sharp-edged rocks and tried not to listen nor to imagine what was happening to her sister and the girls.

Time seemed to stretch, each second a lifetime filled with worry and fear. She licked her lips, choked back a cough, and closed her swollen eyes.

Every tale she had heard about the marauding Paiutes and Bannocks, everything she had read in the newspapers about Little Big Horn and the savages who had massacred General Custer and his troops rushed back to taunt her, to add to her fear. Both hands covering her mouth, Edwina rocked back and forth and fought the scream rising in her throat.

The wind died to a trickle and then returned with a vengeance. Beyond the canyon something exploded, sending out a battering ram of sound. Towering flame brightened the night sky with a billow and surge of unsteady orange light. The acrid smell of smoke wafted down Edwina's hiding place. Men cursed. A woman begged. All while Edwina cowered knowing she could do nothing—except get herself killed or captured. She had to stay alive, to find some way to rescue Olivia from the savages if that were possible. *She had to.*

But the awful silence that followed the crack of mule-skinner whips and the creak of departing wagons was almost as terrifying as the shouting and gunfire. The quiet, broken only by the keening of the wind, told her she was alone in the middle of an unfriendly wilderness.

Cold to the bone, almost ill, Edwina finally roused her unwilling body and searched for a way out of the deep ravine. Clawed by fear and despair, feeling her way through the dense shadows, almost running in the moonlit areas, she stumbled up the canyon. Even after she was sure she had passed the point where she had descended, she continued looking for a gentler way she could ascend with minimal noise.

The bottom of the canyon rose until it was almost level with the surrounding countryside. It left her only a small slope of shifting sand to climb before she trudged on, seeking the camp in a featureless land of sage and rabbit grass and moon-glittered pans of white alkali. Coyotes yipped and sang in the distance. Something large and dark rasped through the sage. Dust caked her face. Sweat, from terror and exertion, ran in muddy trickles down her forehead, and she wiped it away from her stinging eyes. Edwina started to shake when she crested a small sand hill and saw the dying column of spark-laced smoke rising toward a sky that had already lost most of its stars to the argent glow of approaching dawn.

"Dear God, please, no, not Olivia and the girls!" She hadn't the breath to scream the incoherent prayer, but the piteous whisper was surely torn from the aching flesh of her beating heart. Edwina forced her legs to carry her down the hill and across the broad, flat stretch of alkali to what remained of the freight wagons. One was nothing more than a smoldering heap that reeked of strong spirits and burning wool. Another, its contents ransacked, stood where it had been left by the muleskinners. The two-seater waited alone. The rest of the heavy, cumbersome vehicles were gone.

The ominous silence chilled her more than the frosty air of breaking dawn, and she was still trembling violently when she found the first body. It was almost beyond bearing. Edwina clapped her hand over her mouth when she saw the bright blood that covered the whiskery face and head. She was sure he had been scalped.

Not certain which one of the teamsters he was, only certain he was dead, she felt impelled to do something. Cover him up, or say a prayer for the repose of his soul? There wasn't time for that. Fear and despair driving her on, she moved around him and ran, a shambling run that took her first to the wagon that had contained their goods. Her trunk and the rest of their personal effects were relatively un-

26

touched. Whatever the Indians had been looking for, it wasn't a spinster's plain garments, nor the clothes Olivia had been taking to her husband, nor the hams, bacon, beans, spuds, and other edibles the freighters were carrying for their own consumption.

She choked back the whimpers that were crawling up from her pounding heart. Jumping at every sound, every rustle of brush, flap of canvas, every skitter of wind, Edwina picked up a long-bladed knife from beside the dead campfire. She carried it with her as she stumbled on through the silent camp, seeking her sister and the girls.

Dead or alive, the rest of her family was missing. Edwina wouldn't admit it until she had searched the camp twice. She found four male bodies that had been shot, three of them in the blankets where they had spent the night. But the only living creatures in the camp, besides herself, were two large red mules and a dusty-looking gray horse, still saddled and roaming free. She was too dazed to even wonder where it had come from.

The mules were tied to the picket line and seemed as glad to see Edwina as she was to see them. Big Red, the larger of the two mules, eyed her as she approached, but he didn't shy away when she reached out to touch him.

"What am I going to do?" Edwina whispered, staring at the mule. "Help me."

God helps those who help themselves! Martha's oft-repeated words swept through Edwina's mind. She had heard the housekeeper's words a thousand times—and hated them every time—but now she embraced them. If she stood any chance of rescuing her family and getting them all to safety, she needed sense enough to know what to do and how.

"First things first," she told Big Red. "Only what's first? I can't go after them and fight a whole tribe of Indians, I have to . . ." Mouth still open, she stared at the mule for a moment. "Help. I have to find help."

It was a daunting task, one she wasn't at all sure she could handle. But where? Which way? Forward or back? They had to have reached the midpoint of the two hundred miles that separated Winnemucca, Nevada, from Raiter's homestead in Oregon. Their freight wagons had left a track that would lead her back to Winnemucca, and the trail forward bore marks left by other travelers.

Either way, it was a hundred-mile journey across the uninhabited high desert. It was not a journey to be dismissed lightly, or to be undertaken without careful planning, that much she knew. Her ordinarily good sense told her that, but it wasn't sense that was urging her to hurry, to run before the Indians came back, to . . .

His ears back, his eyes intent, Big Red looked beyond her at something that caused him to edge away, jerking at the rope of braided leather that tethered him to the picket line. Eyes staring, teeth bared, the other red mule joined him in his unease. Both had their full attention focused on something in the sagebrush behind her.

At first Edwina thought it was just the wind which had increased in force as the morning light grew stronger. It wasn't the wind. It was an unknown, still-not-visible something that moved slowly, hesitantly, through the sage toward the wagons.

A man crawled out of hiding about twenty feet away and croaked out a word that sounded like "Ed."

Fear squeezing her chest, Edwina whirled and ran toward the blood-crusted, filthy man. It was Shorty, the old muleskinner who had given her his coat and offered her comfort. "Oh, dear God, what have they . . ."

Edwina Parkhurst had been writing of fast guns and

bloody death, under several different names, for a long time, but words on paper in no way prepared her for the true horror of death. Her hands were shaking when she reached out, stopping his forward motion.

She knew Shorty was dying; no one could suffer wounds like his and live. Dropping the knife, she knelt beside him as he collapsed onto the sand. Trying not to weep at the vile, unspeakable damage that had been inflicted on the old man's body, Edwina leaned close, heard his weak whisper, "Hurry, you have to go before . . ."

"Shhh, don't try to talk. I'll get my sister's medicines . . ."

"Please, child, go." Moaning deep in his throat, he took in a shallow breath before he turned his face away. "I'm hurt real bad. I . . . I . . ."

"Indians?" Edwina asked. "Was it Indians that did this?"

"Not Indians."

"Who then?"

There was no answer. Edwina knew, as she heard the sighing exhalation of a final breath, that there would never again be an answer from the old muleskinner. Kneeling still, Edwina fought against the weary numbness that invaded her and the sense of hopelessness that crept into her very soul. She fought until she had regained strength enough to close Shorty's eyes and arrange his limbs in a seemly manner before she got to her feet and went to find a covering for his ravaged body.

That done and a prayer said over him, she stood for a long moment. She tried to quell the emotions gibbering inside her head, telling her that she couldn't possibly make the trip alone. Perhaps it was true, but Edwina couldn't quit. "Just get on with it." Her voice was too loud in the desert stillness, but she continued to talk, telling herself what to do, giving the orders slowly, like a mother to a small child, speaking softly, designating one task at a time. She talked of Olivia, Winnemucca, the girls, whatever came to mind, because she needed to hear the sound of a human voice.

She began the slow task of gathering supplies for the long trip, mentally checking off her needs as she went, and piling the necessary items beside the buggy.

"Ed."

The single word, uttered by an old man's weak voice, clawed its way through the throbbing pain, entered the formless nothing that held Talmadge Jones. It forced him to react, to move his hands toward the twin Colts that were cross-belted around his narrow hips.

There were other words, a two-voiced murmur that was only sound, not sense, as it traveled through the darkness. Within the sound was reassurance. Whoever he was, Ed was just a kid. Not a man. Not danger.

There was no need to draw. Gusting out a sigh, he relaxed his hold on the six-shooters and willed the nothingness to return. It left him alone with his aching head, the total night, and the fragments of memory that were too broken to be coherent. Talmadge Jones shifted his body a little, turned over to his side and tried to sit up. Instead he fell back into the nothingness with a dizzy, sickening swoop. But not before he croaked out the boy's name.

"Ed."

The whisper of sound came from everywhere and nowhere, rasped like the wind in the sage and scraped across her bare nerves like one of Mr. Poe's terror-filled writings, read by lamplight on a dark night.

Gasping, Edwina whirled around, dropped the pile of quilts she was loading into the two-seater, and looked for something to use as a weapon to defend herself.

The gray horse answered the call before she could catch her breath or have the wit to grab the knife she had retrieved from the dirt and put under the front seat of the buggy. Moving away from the picket line, where he had stayed since she unsaddled him and given him and the mules some corn and water, the gelding walked over to the rear of the only remaining freight wagon. There it began nosing the first body she had found and forgotten—the muleskinner who had been scalped.

She was less than a yard away, moving around the gelding, when the man lifted a hand to his bloody head and moaned softly.

He was still alive!

The knowledge filtered slowly in as Edwina stared down at him. Judging from his garments and his cross-belted Colts, he was *not* one of the muleskinners who had driven the wagons from Winnemucca.

She drew the obvious conclusion, linking him with the villains who had killed and destroyed, the outlaws who had taken their plunder and captives and vanished into the wastelands. Edwina took a small step back and tried to control the tremor in her voice. "Who are you? Why have you done this? Where is my sister?"

Groaning again, he said, his voice weak, "Ed? Kid, you have to . . ."

Edwina wanted to—to kill him, maybe. But a touch of remaining reason told her that killing him wouldn't help her rescue Livy and her nieces. The reality of the saddled horse, not an Indian pony, finally penetrated her daze and she realized what Shorty had said. It wasn't Indians who had attacked, and this man was one of the outlaws. She needed to find out what he knew.

"The authorities," she whispered. "I have to take him to the sheriff or somebody in Winnemucca. They'll make him tell what he knows. They'll find Livy and the girls."

Born of desperation, the tentative plan hardened into flinty resolve. It gave her enough courage to shoo the horse out of the way, kneel at the man's side, and examine his wound. A bullet had plowed a bloody diagonal line across his forehead.

Blood and dust had dried to an ugly brown crust on his face. It clung to his whiskers, giving him the appearance of evil. Edwina shuddered, gulped in a breath, and steeled herself to reach out and touch his face to see if he was fevered.

Her fingers had barely grazed his burning cheek when his equally hot hand clamped around her wrist and pulled her close. Choking back a scream, she was almost too frightened to listen. "Thirsty. Water?"

Ignoring his plea, Edwina jerked her wrist free. She remained crouched beside him, trying to remember what little bits of medical knowledge she had garnered over the years. "Think, you blithering idiot. The man has been shot. He has a fever. What are you going to do to keep him alive until you can get him to Winnemucca?"

She frowned at him, asked herself another question. "Laudanum?" She knew it was supposed to dull pain. Without saying why she wanted it, Livy had brought an ample supply with her. She had brought some other medicines too: carbolic salve, papers of sleeping powder, prune syrup, and others. There was bound to be something she could use on the man's wound.

"Thirsty," he said again, struggling to rise.

"Wait," she said, trying unsuccessfully to keep the anger out of her voice as she reluctantly put her hands on his shoulders and pushed him back to the earth. "I need to doctor you first."

He subsided.

With a goal in mind, she got to her feet and hurried to the freight wagon. There, she rummaged through her sister's belongings until she found salve, laudanum, and a length of pink flannel dress goods to tear into washcloths and bandages. Returning to the wounded man, Edwina lifted his head and began to pour a hefty dose of the drug down his throat. Holding his nose when he fought against taking the medicine, she forced him to gulp it down in order to breathe.

That done, she fetched a basin of water and a bar of Livy's precious hard-milled, lily of the valley soap. Without wincing, she cleaned the gaping wound. It was clean and dry when she rubbed on a thick, smelly layer of Dr. Wiseman's Carbolated Salve—guaranteed to cure anything that ails man or beast, its label said—and wound strips of pink flannel around his head. She tied the ends in a granny knot right in the center of his forehead.

It was black dark, not even a speck of light showing, and the wind was kicking up a ruckus, rattling stuff around, throwing grit into his face, and blowing cold.

Whatever the kid had poured down him, it was easing the pain better than any drinking liquor ever would, but it came close to curdling on his tongue, it tasted so foul. Still, the boy was trying to help, and at the moment Talmadge Jones was in need of a big serving of that.

"Kid, you . . . ," he said, the words slurring and sticking to his tongue like mutton grease. He had to warn the boy about the approaching storm. "Listen, boy, there's a storm . . . Got to . . . Hurry . . ."

Smelling of mule and sweat and smoke, and something

else, something female, the boy leaned over him and tried to pull him up. "Come on," the young, slightly husky voice said, "you have to get into the two-seater."

Tal tried, but it was mostly the boy's muscles that got him up on legs that wobbled. He staggered, his weight draped over the kid's shoulders, toward . . . What had the kid called it? A two-seater? A buggy? How did a fancy buggy get out here? He shook his head, or wanted to, while he pondered an even bigger mystery: How could the kid see to lead him anywhere in the black dark?

Wanting to ask for an explanation, but unable to frame the words, Tal let Ed shove him into a padded seat, lift his feet, and wrap something thick and warm around him before the kid tied him snugly in place.

"Thanks, boy," he managed to mumble before he closed his eyes and his mind crawled loose from his body, leaving the rest of him behind in the velvety nothing.

"Boy?" Edwina asked, not talking to the long, lean man slumped and sleeping in the front seat of the yellow-wheeled buggy. His dark whiskers held flecks of his blood, his dusty hair more of the dried flakes, and even with the pink bandage around his head, he still looked dangerous. But not nearly as much as he had before she had eased his Colts out of the holsters and kept them for her own protection. That one word gave her an idea.

If she hadn't been so tired and worried, Edwina Parkhurst might have allowed herself a pang of regret when she hacked off her braid of chestnut hair with the knife. But she was past all that when she traded in her skirts, petticoats, drawers, and corset for the red long johns, wool trousers, and heavy shirt Livy was taking to her beast of a husband.

Wearing the old muleskinner's coat, a sweaty felt hat—she

found it by the burned wagon—and her own Balmoral boots, the newly created Ed Parker let down the side and back curtains on the buggy. She tied them securely in place, picked up the rifle that she was reasonably sure belonged to the outlaw and shoved it under the seat with the knife. She hitched up the two red mules and fastened the gray horse to a lead rope at the rear of the heavily loaded buggy. She headed for Winnemucca with her captive outlaw at her side and a howling, blowing storm hiding the westering sun and pushing her from behind with cold, deadly fingers.

Chapter Four

Edwina was afraid. She had been frightened before, but not like this. If she was any judge of mule behavior, the two mules weren't any better off than she was.

Sighing heavily, she burrowed deeper into the turned-up collar of her coat, trying to keep her nose and mouth free of the blowing sand and alkali dust. Edwina didn't know what to do to save herself or the injured man. Not even in the lurid depths of her imagination could she have conceived such a storm. It was impossible, but it was here, raging across the desert, blowing great billows of icy, blinding sand all around her. It rasped and tore at the canvas covering of the buggy, stung her exposed face, burned her eyes, clogged her nose, and hid everything in sight.

She had been trying to control the fractious mules far too long, making the last hours of travel torture. Her arms and shoulders felt as if all of Satan's minions were poking at them with their fiery pitchforks. Inside the kidskin gloves, her hands were cramped and nearly numb with the strain of gripping the traces.

She sincerely hoped the mules knew where they were going because she couldn't see more than a foot in any direction. It was so cold that Edwina, despite the feel of the unseemly and unfamiliar male garments, was thankful for the warmth and comfort the long johns and trousers provided her. They were aided by the thick wool blanket she had wrapped around herself and the laudanum-dosed outlaw. She had stopped before the worst of the storm hit to rest the mules and find something to cover the outlaw's exposed face. He was her only hope of saving her sister, and she wanted him alive.

"We should have been there by now," she muttered. "It can't have been more than nine or ten miles back from where we camped for the night."

She was bone-tired but her mind was still working. She remembered the noon stop of the day before, remembered distinctly the narrow, gaping mouth of the high-walled canyon that yawned just beyond the site. She remembered, too, Shorty telling her the canyon was haunted by the ghosts of dead Paiutes.

"That's why the Paiutes ain't wintering in there anymore. Why, they up and left after a bunch of 'em sickened and died back in that canyon. It's a nice camping place, too. I spent me a night or two in that lodge—them hot springs do a good job warming old bones. Hell, even sheepherders are smart enough to know that. One of 'em, before he got his fool self kilt, was talking about setting up camp in there permanent," he had said, winking at the girls as he went on talking about winter lodges and smoke holes and sweating out demons. Edwina had listened and wanted to explore the canyon, but Livy's frown and sniff of disapproval at the heathenish tales had sent the old man back to more congenial companions.

With no other option, Edwina was hoping he hadn't been yarning, that the abandoned Indian camp actually existed. Even if it didn't, the canyon walls would provide some measure of protection from the wind.

"Mules is smart," Shorty had told her when he was teaching her to harness the beasts and to drive the buggy before they left Winnemucca. "Leave 'em be and they'll get back to the barn, or wherever it be that they can find a mite of comfort."

Edwina prayed that was true, that the mules would find the canyon and get them to a place of safety before it was too late. And soon, because it felt like the sand had been joined by pellets of ice.

Despite Edwina's prayers to the contrary, within minutes the storm worsened. She lifted a hand to swipe at the flakes of snow that were catching in her eyelashes. A wheel dropped into a hole and the buggy lurched sideways. She grabbed for the outlaw to keep from sliding, and the mules chose that moment to jerk the reins out of her hand. Spooked by wind and storm, Rude and Big Red bolted.

Attached to the mules by harness and chain, the two-seater—with Edwina frantically hanging onto the outlaw—followed, helplessly and wildly. The buggy bounced, leaped, jolted, and bumped along behind the mules.

Thrown back and forth, up and down, Edwina was sure she was going to be tossed from the carriage and left behind to freeze in the desert. Thankful she had had the foresight to tie him to the seat, she clung to the stranger with desperate determination.

Feeling almost gone from her hands and arms, choking on alkali dust, she was still clinging to him when the dangerous ride ended abruptly in a crash, followed by a tearing, breaking sound. The buggy tilted alarmingly, settled, partially then came to a dead stop. It all happened so quickly that Edwina was flung forward with brutal force.

Her death grip on the man was broken. She almost toppled out on the squealing, thrashing mules. She would have if her legs hadn't gotten tangled in the blanket, jerking her onto her knees on the floor of the buggy behind the inward curve of the dash. Her upper half was hanging over, numb arms dangling toward Rude and Red and their noisy struggle to regain their feet.

"Kid? Kid?" Even slurred by laudanum, the man's voice was deep and just a little scared, too. "Kid, are you all right? What happened? What's making that racket?"

When she didn't answer immediately, he said, "Damn it, kid, say something."

Despite the fact that he was a killer, had taken a part in her sister's abduction, and was probably more depraved than she could possibly imagine, the concern in his voice was comforting.

It put a little starch in her wilting backbone. She would handle this—just like she had handled every other crisis in her life since she had left the schoolroom and become the family caretaker. Of course, this was her first life or death crisis.

Moving slowly, she straightened and climbed back onto the cushioned seat. Leaning close enough so that he could hear her over the squealing mules, she gave him a condensed version of the trials and tribulations of Ed Parker and the runaway mules.

Ed finished the short recital, "The mules are down and tangled in the harness. I have to cut them loose before they hurt themselves."

Climbing out of the shelter of the buggy wasn't anything she wanted to do, but she didn't have a choice. She couldn't let the poor beasts suffer. Fumbling through the welter of objects she had tossed onto the floorboards she found the knife. With body-aching reluctance, she climbed out of the buggy which had a pronounced tilt, the outlaw's side now the low end.

There was something around his throbbing head, obstructing his sight and muffling sound. Tal figured the kid had put the thick covering on to protect him from the hellish storm. He was grateful, in a sort of addled, not quite coherent fashion. He ought to be helping the boy with the downed animals but for some reason he couldn't move.

Pondering, he had a vague recollection of being shot and of the kid pouring a dose of something bitter down his gullet. But it didn't seem likely that those two things were tying him to what felt like a padded seat. A buggy? Did he remember the kid saying something about a buggy? Tal shook his head. Nothing was making a whole lot of sense.

"Kid?" he said. "Don't . . ." He lost whatever else he was going to say and he dozed. He woke with a start, listened intently and heard nothing but the storm, which unnerved him. By all rights, there should have been noise. Screaming mules. A husky-voiced kid that sounded scared and exhausted.

Where was the kid? Didn't he say he was going to cut the mules loose? Mules were mean, ornery buzzards, especially if they were hurting. Had the fool kid been mule-kicked? Was he lying out in the storm, needing help? Tal struggled to move, but whatever held him in place was stubborn and gave no slack.

Ropes? Was that what was wrapped tight around him? Tal shook his head and pain slammed into it like another bullet. He gasped and tried to lift one hand, wanting to cradle the ache, but his arms were bound against his body.

"Kid? Ed? Where are you?"

There was no reply. He waited, fighting the pain, and tried again, "Damn it, kid, answer me." It sounded a lot weaker and a whole lot madder, but it still didn't get him an answer.

But it did get him another strong dose of swooping darkness and disjointed bits and scraps of information, most of it meaningless. Sand and alkali dust gritted between his teeth and mixed with the biting aftertaste of whatever painkiller the kid had poured down his throat. His nose was clogged with dust, but oddly enough, not even that could hide the faint odor of violets that emanated from his head covering.

Had he heard a woman screaming when he rode into the muleskinners' camp? It seemed like it, but that didn't make any sense either. What would a woman be doing out in the desert at this time of year, especially with several wagon loads of whiskey? Befuddled, drifting closer and closer to darkness, Tal mentally shook his head. He tried to grasp the elusive memory of a woman who might be Raiter's wife. The effort pushed him over the edge and he tumbled back into the nothingness pit. He regained a smattering of sense when the canted buggy shifted, creaked, and made a grinding noise when someone climbed in over the top of the inward curving, nearly waist-high dash.

"Kid? That you?"

Her thigh a burning ache from a mule kick, her body shaking with cold, Edwina heard the outlaw's question, but she had neither the breath nor the inclination to answer. What was there to say?

"I've been creeping around the buggy forever? Trying to do things by feel alone? The horse is gone? The mules are gone? The buggy is wedged tight between what feels like some trees and rocks? I think it's broken beyond repair? We're stranded in the desert and are probably going to freeze to death? I'm so tired I can't think, scared silly, and don't know what to do?"

It was all true, but she was too tired and discouraged to give it voice.

"Ed, is that you?"

"Yes."

"The mules? Did they . . ."

Feeling churlish, and sort of enjoying it, she said, "They're gone. Go back to sleep."

"The storm?"

Relenting a little, she said, "It's black night, and I can't tell for sure where we are, but the wind isn't as strong. There's hardly any sand blowing, but it feels like it's snowing hard and it's cold."

"We can't do much until morning, kid," he said, his voice slurring again, "and you sound beat. Why don't you rest some and when it gets light, we can see what . . ."

At that moment, more than anything else in the world, Edwina wanted to drop on the buggy seat and fall asleep, but she couldn't. He was an outlaw, a lawless, murdering who-knows-what, but he was still a human being. She couldn't leave him to die; she had to keep them both alive. That meant protecting them from the storm. She knew she was going to have to untie him, give him a chance to survive even if she didn't. He might be a killer of helpless humans, but she wasn't. And she was too tired and cold to embark on a new career.

Moving slowly, shivering, Edwina cut the ropes that held the outlaw, but only after she had dosed him with laudanum again. Using the last of her strength she dragged the rest of the blankets and pillows from of the rear seat and spread them out. Covering them from head to toe, wedging the pillows around their legs and against the canvas on his side of the seat, she hoped their combined warmth would add protection from the cold.

Not even in that tiny space of sense could Edwina Parkhurst, spinster, admit that she needed to be close to him, to know that she was not totally alone in the untamed wilderness. She didn't try to move when warmth seeped into her shaking body and sleep took some of the weariness from her muscle and bone. She relaxed against him solid and alive beside her.

Whatever the kid kept feeding him was powerful stuff. It kept the ache in his head off at a distance, but it sure came carrying extra baggage.

Ed was a boy, and just a kid at that. A kid who smelled strongly of mules and sweat, certainly not like any woman Tal had ever met. He had tended Tal's gunshot wound, likely saved his life.

"Damn it, kid," he muttered, "what have you done to me?" The sound was lost in the moaning of the storm. Tal knew nothing more until sleep, and the odd, vaguely troubling dreams that lurked there, released him.

The buggy seat still sloped, but it was the quiet and the cold that woke him. The ear-aching quiet of snow piled deep and growing deeper, but it wasn't snow that caused him worry. It was the cold where the sleeping kid should have been, but wasn't.

Tal hadn't heard or felt Ed leave the buggy, but he did hear something walking around, softly crunching the snow. It sounded bigger than the kid. That sent a shiver of fear racing up his backbone and his hands reaching for the Colts that should have been on his hips, but weren't.

Still groggy but on the edge of mad, Tal eased the blanket off his head and stared out into the black night. Snowflakes, soft and cold, whispered onto his face, touched his alkali-dried lips. He caught one on his tongue and knew his earlier guess had been correct: it was snowing hard. And the kid was out there in the storm and night. The kid and whatever was walking around, moving closer to the buggy.

Knowing he had to do something, Tal began to free him-

43

self from the load of blankets the kid had heaped on him. He was down to the last one and ready to climb out of the buggy when Ed asked, "What are you doing?"

Hoarseness growling through his voice made him sound mean. Talmadge Jones snarled, "Where in the hell are my guns? There's something sneaking up on us and I . . ."

"What are you talking about? There's nothing . . ."

Tal tried to stand up but dizziness held him down. "Damn it, kid, I can hear it and . . ."

"Don't be a fool! It's just your horse. He came back and is . . ."

"You don't know that," he snapped, anger knotting up in his belly, tasting sour in his throat.

"Of course I do," Ed said, his snarl a match for Tal's. "You would, too, if you'd just look."

"Look? Kid, it's black night, how can I . . ." Tal's fists unclenched. His right hand came up to feel his face. He fingered the bandage the kid had tied around his head, wincing as his touch gave new life to the pain that waited there, and rubbed at his eyes. They were gummy with sleep and had accumulated a fair amount of dust from the storm, but they were open.

Open and seeing nothing but night. "It's morning then? Daylight?" he asked, marveling at the calmness in the simple question.

"Yes. What's the matter?"

He didn't want to answer, but he did. "I can't see a blasted thing."

The kid was quiet for a long time before he said, his voice softer, "You were shot in the head. That's probably what caused it."

Despite the feeling that was distancing him from pain and understanding, Tal grimaced.

Sounding scared and wary, the kid was still a little distance from the buggy when he asked, "What's funny?"

"Me," Tal answered. "It's for damned sure that I'll have to find me a new way to make a living."

"What?"

Tal asked, "What do you think, kid? Would anybody in their right mind hire a blind gunfighter?"

"I think you're raving," Ed said, his voice flat except for what might have been a tinge of fear. "Your fever is probably up again, and you need another dose of laudanum."

"Will it help me see again?"

"How do I know? I'm not a doctor," he retorted, moving closer. "But you being blind won't matter a bit if I can't find us some shelter and some heat before night."

"Are things that bad?"

"Worse," Ed said. His voice held nothing but weariness and truth.

Chapter Five

Blind! The single word seemed to hover in the snow-filled air, drawing her close enough to see the shock and fear he was trying to hide behind his attempt at carelessness. Uncertain of her own feelings, Edwina stopped beside the wrecked buggy, watching the outlaw as he struggled with the knowledge of his blindness.

The man was a criminal, in cahoots with the men who had abducted her sister and nieces. Everything about him, from the wolfish cast of his face to his yellowish-brown eyes, warned her that he was dangerous. She didn't want to feel any compassion for him.

Weariness, lack of sleep, hunger, grief and the aftermath of fear—it all combined to overwhelm her.

The gunslinger was sightless, and bad as that was, it wasn't even close to being the worst of her problems. The only good thing she could think of was that the horse, who had broken loose from the back of the buggy sometime during their wild ride, was back and seemed glad to be in their company. With the food she had brought, they would have drinking water from the little stream running somewhere nearby. If she could find somewhere to build a fire and cook. Raw beans and bacon didn't sound appetizing, even if there was plenty of water to wash them down with.

Clearing her throat, Edwina remembered just in time to add a bit of boyishness to her voice. "Mister, I have to . . ."

"Call me Tal, kid," he said, interrupting her mid-sentence. "Talmadge Jones, late of points north and heading straight for hell—which, by all accounts I've heard, is a damn sight warmer than it is here."

Edwina knew he was introducing himself and trying to ease his own shock and pain with a joke. "Ed," she said in return, and added, "Ed Parker. I have to do some exploring. The buggy's wheel is busted and there are big holes in the side-curtains. We'll freeze here so I have to try to find us a place that's sheltered enough to at least build a fire."

"Where are we?" He tried to get out of the buggy seat but sat back down with a little more force than he had evidently thought was probable. Grabbing his head with both hands, Tal let fly with a string of curses.

She didn't respond. Instead she looked at the rugged wall of stone beside the wrecked buggy. It rose high enough to be lost in the swirl of falling snowflakes and the pale watery light of the stormy day. There was no climbing that. Its twin, equally dark and forbidding, was barely visible on the opposite side of what had to be a deep, narrow canyon.

Too tired to allow more than a vague hint of hope to creep into her voice, Edwina said, "From the way it looks, we're in a canyon of some sort. Shorty said there was an abandoned Indian camp in one near where we made our noon stop day before yesterday, and I was heading there when the mules . . ."

Tal tried to clamber out of the buggy again and almost pitched facedown into the snow. Catching him by the arm and pushing him back onto the buggy seat, Edwina didn't try to keep the irritation out of her voice. "Get back under the blankets and keep as warm as you can while I go and see what's around the corner."

He didn't argue, just sort of slumped down on the padded seat and practically wheezed out the single word, "Shorty?"

Edwina took in a breath, wincing a little as the cold air knifed into her chest. Her voice betrayed far too much when she said, "One of the muleskinners with—with . . . He—he died like the rest of them."

"A skinner was killed? On Raiter's whiskey train?" His voice was sharper and blood had come back to his face, tinting what she could see of his skin with a rosy glow that spoke of continued fever. "What else happened? How did you escape?"

She didn't answer immediately. She couldn't—there were too many questions racing through her mind—and she certainly didn't intend to confess her sin to a murderous stranger. But questions remained and they needed answers. Whiskey? What was Ambrose going to do with a mule train-load of whiskey? Jones had to be mistaken. Why would he . . .

At the moment, the questions had no answers, and Edwina, despite her confusion about Raiter and the whiskey, knew she had no time to pry more information from the outlaw.

"It's not snowing quite so hard and I have to see if I can find some shelter." Without looking back to see if he had returned to the nest of blankets and using the canyon wall as her guide, she took several steps toward her goal.

"Ed? Ed?" Tal called, loud enough to stir a few echoes from the canyon walls. "The Indian camp. Do you know what to look for?"

Of course she didn't. Edwina Parkhurst had never written about any kind of Indian dwellings except tipis, and she was fairly certain they weren't what she was looking for.

"Look for mounds," he said. "Paiute winter lodges are covered with tule mats and mud. Round on top. Dug down in . . ."

Edwina turned. There was a veil of falling snow between

48

her and the buggy, but that didn't keep her from seeing that he had fallen sideways on the seat and was shaking fiercely. Of course, he hadn't covered up. She had to make sure he didn't freeze to death. He was her captive, and she darned sure wasn't going to let him die. He probably needed it, but she didn't dare give him any more of the laudanum—not if she intended to move him to some sort of shelter. He had to be able to help. She sighed, but her hands were gentle when she wrapped the outlaw warmly. "I'll be back as soon as I can."

"Be careful, kid," he said, the sound not much more than a rasping whisper. "Real careful. The Paiutes and Bannocks are off the reservation and raising hell. Use my guns if you have to, but try and make sure they don't see you first."

"Mr. Jones, you have to help me."

Tal felt the kid tugging at him, heard the worry in the husky voice, and tried to cooperate but couldn't seem to do much more than wiggle. He tried again, managed to open his eyes and looked toward the kid's voice. He dragged the words out of the burning haze that gripped him, "You find the Indian lodges?"

"No. It's starting to snow harder. Please, try to get up. We have to go."

He gathered his strength and sat upright. Breathing hard from the effort, he asked, "Where?"

"It's a stable, I think. There's a lot of hay. It's built against the canyon wall and . . ."

Faint and fuzzy came memories of a tale he'd heard once about a sheepherder. He didn't want to shake his head, didn't want the pain to come stampeding back, but he did. Something about the memory was important and he had to . . .

Tal shook his head again and groaned, biting back the

49

string of curses that waited in his mouth. Cussing took energy and he didn't have any to spare. "Stable?" he asked, his hands coming up to hold his throbbing head. "What kind of stable?"

"Mr. Jones, please. We don't have time to . . ."

He had to solidify the distorted memories that were crawling back, one by one, but not attaching to each other. "Kid, stable? Please."

"Rock with some kind of mud or something for a top. Not great big, but big enough for us and the horse. Someone cut a lot of hay and piled it inside. There's a rock wall around a fair-sized corral or something. I don't know. It's a place where we can get out of the storm."

The kid sounded muley, but Tal felt like grinning. It came close to being a miracle, but if what he was thinking was true, then the kid had really counted coup on this one.

The sheepherder had been in Raiter's saloon, whiskey-bragging about the valley he was fixing to homestead. A valley with a medium-sized Paiute winter lodge in good shape, hot springs for bathing, and a stable made of stone, topped with willow sticks and tule mats the man had said. Just before he was caught dealing from the bottom of the deck and had gone to meet his maker holding four aces and a trey of hearts. This canyon where they were could be just what the poor idiot had been talking about.

"Mr. Jones, it's cold. I've got your horse here. If you'd just try and . . ."

The kid was nagging him and pulling him at the same time, distracting his thoughts from dead sheepherders. It took a lot of pushing and cajoling on Ed's part to get Tal on top of the gelding. But he was riding bareback and hanging on clumsily as the kid led the way into the valley.

Snow was wet and soothing on his face. It took away some

of the fever that was turning him to ash. Tal licked his lips, sucking in the moisture with a thirst that burned as hot as the fever. He repeated the act again and again until the edge was gone from the thirst. It was only held at bay for the moment, but that was enough because then he remembered.

"The lodge," he said. "Look for it. It's our best chance. It's made out of long willow branches stuck in the ground and curved over toward the other side, making a sort of half-circle sticking out of the ground. Covered with tule mats and mudded over. Lots of wood in there. He said . . ."

"Who said? Mr. Jones, who said something about this place? Was it Shorty? Did you know . . ."

Tal bent lower over the horse's neck and tried to remember what it was he had been trying to say. His waning strength took away thought and left only the dogged will to stay on the gelding until the kid hauled him down and dumped him somewhere. He hoped it was somewhere close because otherwise he wasn't sure he was going to make it.

It hadn't been easy. Without the heavy snowfall letting up for a few moments, allowing some visibility, it wouldn't have been possible at all. But she had found it. Not sure he wouldn't fall into the growing snowdrift outside the lodge opening, Edwina pulled at him, felt him stir, and, with new fear tightening its hold on her mind, also felt the heat that emanated from him. He was burning up with fever.

Right now, the first thing was to look inside the Indian dwelling and see if it was going to be a better shelter than the stone stable. Shaking his arm, she said, "Mr. Jones, I found the lodge like you said and I need to look inside, to see if we can stay in there or not. Please, try not to fall off the horse until I get back."

"Yeah. Kid, I . . . thanks." He raised his head, turned his

blind eyes in her general direction, and licked his lips. "Hurry."

Edwina ducked through the opening into the lodge, struck one of the lucifer matches she had brought with her and held it high. Dug down into the earth about two feet, floored with flat stones, the lodge seemed to be snug and whole, and about half-filled with dry wood. She breathed a silent thankful prayer as she touched a second match to the bone-dry firewood and fluffs of tinder that were laid and ready in the fire pit dug out in the center of the floor.

Orange flame leaping and cavorting, the fire was roaring in an instant, sending out heat and light, already starting to warm the reasonably large, dome-shaped lodge. Coated with snow, hurting in more places than she knew she had, all she had time to think about was getting the outlaw off the horse and into the warmth before she took the horse and started ferrying their supplies to the lodge. It all had to be done and the horse had to be cared for before she could even think about changing into something warm and dry, eating, and getting some rest.

It was a long time, but she managed to finish before darkness and blowing storm conquered the valley. The horse was rubbed dry, covered with one of Olivia's best wool blankets, watered, fed, and bedded in dried meadow grass up to his hocks. Talmadge Jones was dosed with laudanum, his head salved and rebandaged, his belly filled with fried ham and pan bread, washed down with gallons of water. Edwina had been too tired to even blush when she stripped him to the hide, seeing a few sights spinsters aren't usually privileged to observe, and clothed him in the spare union suit she found in his bedroll. She had discovered it still tied behind the saddle she had thrown into the buggy with the rest of the supplies she had brought from the camp.

She didn't even glance in his direction or feel the slightest shame when she undressed before the fire, crawled into a clean pair of long johns, and tumbled into the snug pallet she had spread on the stone floor beside Tal's. It was warm and comfortable beyond belief, made so by the sheepskins she had discovered piled in the lodge.

The sound of the coffee grinder and the smell of fresh-ground beans woke him. The pain in his head only a lurking beast like the horror of his blindness, Tal lay there trying to piece together bits of fevered memories. He needed to sort through what was truth and what had to be demons from his own mind.

He knew time had passed—it was just how much that set him to wondering. It might have been a week or longer, he didn't know for sure. He only knew the kid had been there, yelling at him, ordering him to stay alive, forcing him to eat mashed beans and drink water, dosing him with bitter draughts of painkiller. The kid got him up to walk out into the storm to answer his natural needs and tended him with gentle hands.

It was the memory of the hands touching his face, washing his fevered body with coolness, holding him when the demons attacked that troubled him. Before he could stop himself, he asked, his voice crawling out of his mouth slow, lazy, and only slightly slurred. "How long you been swamping for the muleskinners, kid? They teach you how to make coffee?"

Sounding huffy, the kid said, "I'm not a swamper. Martha taught me how to make coffee, not that it's all that hard to do."

"So they say," Tal said. "Now me, I always have a hankering for it, but it either comes out like tar or hasn't got a leg to stand on. Maybe Martha can teach me. Is she waiting for you back in Winnemucca?"

Listening carefully, Tal heard the glug of water as the kid filled the coffeepot and the crunch and snap of fire and wood as he set it in the coals. And ham, judging from the mouth-watering odor it was sending out, was sizzling in a pan before the boy answered. "No, she isn't in Winnemucca. She's back home with my mother and aunt and I wish . . ."

In one those moments when his ears and brain weren't trotting together, Tal did a little wandering that edged close to falling back into nothingness. He was sitting propped up and leaning against something soft when the kid put a cup of coffee in his hands and told him to be careful drinking it. He took a sip, managing to find his mouth on the first try, and then took another, savoring the rich taste. The cup was empty when he said, "Kid, that's the best coffee I ever tasted. You sure your Martha wouldn't like to teach me the how of making it?"

"Very sure."

Under a strong hint of Southern heritage, Ed's husky voice spoke of schools and books and gentlefolk that added to Tal's curiosity. "Well, if you aren't a swamper, what were you doing on the desert with the train?" Suddenly aware of his actions, Tal closed his mouth. It wasn't healthy to question another man.

"I was with my sister," Ed said slowly. "Her husband sent for her and the preacher made her come because it was her Christian duty to obey her husband. I came to take care of— of . . ."

It sounded like the boy was trying to keep from crying and that touched Talmadge Jones in an unfamiliar place. It's that damned medicine, he told himself. It's making you maudlin. In less than a minute, you'll be bawling like a weaning calf.

No matter what he told himself nothing could stop him

from asking, "Who's your sister? What kind of bastard is she married to that would have her traveling out here this time of year?"

"Her name's Olivia. She's married to Ambrose Raiter."

The kid's words came out flat, like Ed wouldn't be doing much crying if Raiter was gut-shot and lying in the dirt. Tal found enough sense not to tell the kid that he had been riding out to meet the train because Ambrose Raiter had hired him. Ed might not have much feeling for Raiter, but they were still kin.

So, instead of putting his foot in his mouth, Tal said, choosing his words carefully, "I thought I heard a woman back there, just before I was shot. Where is she? God, kid, I'm a fool." He couldn't make his tongue stop wagging. "You said whoever jumped the wagon train killed the skinners. They didn't kill her, too, did they?"

"Damn you," the kid said, hate harsh in his voice. "I hope you rot in hell for what . . . Olivia and the girls didn't do anything. They're not much more than babies and . . ."

Shocked, Tal took a deep breath. "Little girls?"

"Not real little, one's fifteen and the other is almost thirteen. Meg and Becca. My nieces. Olivia's daughters. Your gang took them. I don't . . ."

"My gang?" Talmadge Jones tried to absorb this new information. The kid obviously thought he was involved with whoever it was that ambushed the wagon train and kidnapped Raiter's wife and daughters as well as his whiskey.

"Kid," he said, talking into a dark silence broken only by the fire noises and the faraway howl of a rising wind, "I'll swear by any god you want that I had nothing to do with the attack on the camp. I just walked in and was shot for my trouble. I don't know who was there or what happened."

There was a stirring in the air, a whisper of draft. The

scent of frying ham came strong to Tal's nostrils, ham and coffee and a faint whiff of violets. If the boy was still in the lodge, he was neither moving nor talking.

Chapter Six

Crouching beside the fire pit, staring across to where Talmadge Jones was sitting, Edwina fought back the tears that ached in her throat. Was Tal lying about not being with the gang that had attacked the wagon train? Why else would he have been out there in the desert?

Even if he was a gunfighter, he didn't have to be a murdering outlaw. Or so her fickle mind tried to tell her—the same mind that had given birth to her own gunfighter, Lobo Chance, and forgave him for his many sins because he fought on the side of right, not might. That didn't mean Talmadge Jones was cut from the same bolt of material as Lobo Chance. Did it?

A new storm was beginning to blow outside, pushing at the blanket she had hung over the entrance, stirring up the pungent sheep-sage-and-smoke tainted air inside the lodge. It was the third storm that had roared through the valley in the ten days they had been there. She could hear it lashing and wailing, as fierce as the storm that raged inside her head.

Tal was an outlaw, one of the murderous gang that had killed Shorty and the others. If he wasn't, if he was just another victim of that terrible night, what would she do? If he didn't know where they had taken her sister, couldn't tell the sheriff in Winnemucca, how in the name of God could she even hope to save Olivia and the girls? Odd as it seemed, as much as she loved her sister and nieces, Edwina didn't want Talmadge Jones to be one of that gang.

She took in a shuddering breath and tried not to feel, not to be afraid. But the fear was still heavy when she straightened and added a few more lengths of split juniper chunks to the fire. Stirring the coals, she watched the leap of the flame as it danced high, reflected off the fire-smoked, curving dome of their surprisingly comfortable dwelling. A warm comfort that was at least partially helped by the snow that had fallen thick and deep.

Her meandering thoughts added another small fact: The runoff from the hot spring in the smaller lodge, the one she thought of as the bathhouse or the washroom where she washed the grime from their clothing, certainly wasn't covered in snow. It was easier to let her thoughts dwell on steaming mineral water bubbling up in a rocky pool, hot baths, and washing clothes, than it was to worry. Talmadge Jones had been occupying a large share of her thoughts for almost two weeks and he was likely to keep on doing so until . . .

"Kid? I didn't mean to . . ."

Startled, Edwina jumped and swallowed back a betraying cry. Whether he was involved with the gang or not, she couldn't let him know she wasn't a boy. A sob sneaked out before she could grab it back. At the small sound, Tal sat up straighter, acting like he was planning to crawl out of his sickbed and come looking for her.

"Kid? Where in hell are you? What's wrong?"

"I'm here," she snapped, poking at the fire again. A gust of icy air found its way into the room, making her gratefully aware of the trousers that covered her lower limbs before it roiled the smoke from the fire and escaped through the hole in the roof.

Her mind was on the fear that had been her constant companion for what seemed an eternity. Fear that had changed as circumstances demanded, encompassed immediate concerns, but always was there. It sneered at her, told her Talmadge Jones was going to die, that she was going be left all alone in the desert. When he was raving, when she had to hold him down to wash his fevered body, she had come very close to believing the fear.

Now that he sounded like he might be going to live, her fear reverted back to its origins. Back to Olivia and the girls and what had happened that terrible night. It was that fear that said, "Mr. Jones, I thought that men in the West always treated women with . . ."

She took a deep breath and steadied her voice. "Why did those men take my sister and the girls? What are they going to do to . . ." She couldn't allow herself to finish either the question or the thought.

"I don't know what's going to happen to them." He paused and Edwina could almost hear him picking through his possible responses. What Tal finally said surprised her.

"Men are men, kid," he said. "Some of them treat women like ladies, others . . ." He took a deep breath and went on, his deep voice faintly slurred, still showing the effect of the laudanum. "There was talk that your sister's husband was . . . I shouldn't be doing the talking, but I reckon you know Raiter's mean. He takes what he wants. Kid, he's hurt some women, forcing them into a profession that's . . ."

There was a moment of silence, a brief time when even the wind seemed to be holding its breath. Or maybe Edwina was so intent on his words that she imputed her own motives to the storm. She leaned forward and waited.

"I know you're a tenderfoot, kid, and are finding things different here than where you're from, but are you old enough to understand what I'm trying to tell you?"

"Calico queens?" she asked. She knew what they were, had read enough to know that some women sold their bodies for men's pleasure. But as a maiden lady discussing this subject with a man, Edwina blamed the heat of the fire for the glow that burned her cheeks—even if Tal couldn't see her blushing.

"That's right. Raiter even promised one who works upstairs over his saloon a fancy new two-seater. He was going to have it sent up from Winnemucca and . . ."

Edwina's harsh laugh was brittle and verging on tears. "And I wrecked it good and proper. That's one fancy buggy that Ambrose Raiter won't be giving to a fancy woman."

Tal didn't see much to laugh about in their present predicament. "Is that what we were riding in when the mules . . . You drove it?"

"Yes, and my sister, Ambrose's legal wife, rode beside me the whole way. She wouldn't have, if she . . ."

"The women aren't all bad, kid. Most of them are just doing whatever they can to get by and they didn't set out to end that way. The ones upstairs at Raiter's are . . ."

What he was saying finally penetrated her brain. "Are you telling me that Olivia's husband is running a saloon and a—a . . . Livy thought . . . she's going to be . . . uh . . . very unhappy. He told her he had homesteaded a piece of land."

"He's got a homestead all right, but, kid, you'd better believe there's more money in whiskey and women and faro than sod busting," Tal said slowly. "Lots more money. Talk was Raiter's wife was coming out to give him some respectability. He wants to enter politics."

"The bastard!"

Tal lifted one hand to the pink flannel bandage that decorated his head, grimaced, and eased his long body back onto the bed she had fashioned of sheepskins, blankets, and two of Livy's big goosedown pillows.

Swallowing hard, trying to rid herself of the acrid taste of fear and rage, Edwina changed the subject. "We can't do anything about Raiter now, so I guess we'd better just . . . Mr. Jones, are you hungry? I have no idea what time it is, but the beans are done. The ham's fried and I made some hoecake to go with the molasses."

"Kid, there's something. I don't know whether it'll help or not, since I don't know who took your sister or why, but there were whispers concerning one of the women Raiter forced. She was young, just a little girl really, not old enough to be willing. Her father was up in Idaho mining country. He came back right after she killed herself. The father like to went crazy when he found the girl. Kid, I'm not saying it was him, but that wagon train was loaded down with rotgut whiskey, Raiter's whiskey, and your sister was . . ."

He was breathing hard. The ruddy firelight touched his face, glistened on his whiskers, turned each drop of sweat to beads of blood. Worried, Edwina took a step toward the bottle of laudanum, but Tal, as if he could read her intentions from the sound of her feet, waved her back. "No painkiller. Not yet," he said "I have to tell you."

He sucked in a breath and pushed himself up, staring blindly. "Kid, I know what you're thinking and if there's killing to be done when my sight comes back, I'll put my hands and my guns in your service."

"You don't owe . . ."

"I owe you, but owing you has nothing to do with what I'm promising."

After he had been silent for a long time, Edwina poured another cup of coffee from the blackened pot, added a little melted snow water to cool it down, and carried it to where he sat, leaning back against the wall. "Here," she said, her voice soft, "drink this."

He held the tin cup in both hands and brought it to his mouth. The coffee warmed his dry throat and kept him from talking about things better left unsaid. He didn't know what was prompting him, but now, when it was too damned late, he was starting to feel, to need, and to want. First, he would see the kid safe in Winnemucca and he had to stay alive long enough to do it.

"Kid," he said, "I'd be grateful for a plate of that grub. I'm feeling lank." He tried to ease some of the tension even a blind man could see in the lodge. "I reckon I've been too busy catching up on my sleep to do justice to your cooking."

Ed helped him eat, and washed the mess off his face and out of his whiskers afterwards without complaining. Tal swallowed the painkiller and didn't make a face, settling back into his bed when the kid told him to.

Still, it was disturbing when the kid put a hand on Tal's forehead to see if he was still fevered, and the hand was soft enough to belong to a woman. The hand disappeared, but the scent of violets followed him into his dreams. What sounded like scratching brought him to a slow awakening. He lay there for a long time, trapped in his own darkness, listening. He knew the kid was making the sound, but what in the hell was Ed doing?

It sounded like a pen scratching on paper. After listening for a time longer, Tal asked, his voice sounding as lazy and comfortable as he felt, "Kid, what are you doing?"

The scratching stopped. A silence followed, broken finally by the kid's terse, almost embarrassed, "Writing."

Writing? Tal pondered the word. "Writing what?" he

asked, expecting the kid to say he was writing a letter to his mother.

"A book."

That was a stopper, the kid writing a book. Tal chuckled, thinking he was joining in the joke. "What kind of book, kid? A dime novel?"

"Yes."

Ordinarily, he was a prudent man, a man who knew better than to poke around where he had no business. Talmadge Jones broke a whole host of his own rules. "Why?"

"Why not?" Ed answered, sounding peevish. There was a moment of silence and then the scratching began again, and even it seemed out of sorts.

"Sorry, kid," he said, meaning it. "I wish I could blame that stuff you've been pouring down my throat, but the truth is, I was just plain being nosy."

The scratching stopped, but the quiet got painful before the kid said, "I'm writing because I have to. I promised Beadle and Adams, a company that publishes dime novels, that I would send them four books while I was out here with my sister. I still have to keep my word."

Tal was puzzled. "How long have you been writing?"

"Forever," Ed answered, and then he sighed before adding, "It's been a secret for a long time. I suppose it doesn't matter now."

"Why?" Tal wasn't sure he was asking why it had been a secret or why it didn't matter, but it seemed important to ask.

"After my father got killed, someone had to support the family. I was the only one able to do so. My mother, aunt, and sister are Christian women. According to their preacher, dime novels and the rest of the small books are the devil's snares for the weak and innocent, leading their readers straight to hell. Back at the camp, Livy found out what I was doing. She tore up what I had written, threw it down in a ravine, and told me I had shamed the family. I went down to get my writing and I was so mad at her that I stayed down there all night. That's why the outlaws didn't kill me, too. They were looking for me but I . . ."

Before Tal could do much more than clear his throat, Ed continued. "Livy's a moral woman who will insist on telling everyone about me after she's rescued. Even if my writing kept them out of the poorhouse, my family will be terribly shamed to learn what I've been doing to keep them housed and fed. They'll pray for my eternal soul, Mr. Jones, but I doubt very much that they will ever forgive me."

It didn't sound like the kid was feeling sorry for himself. It was more like he was stating a fact, recounting a truth he had known and already accepted.

Not bothering to mince words, Tal said, "When it comes to being stupid and ungrateful, being men or women doesn't seem to make a whole lot of difference, does it?"

"I suppose not."

The scratching started again, stopped. Restless, tired of the pallet, even if it was comfortable, Tal turned to his side. He was amazed at the lack of pain in his head, but what almost stopped his breath was the glimmer of light he could see. Pale, fuzzy, practically non existent, it was there for a second or two and then it faded to not-quite-black. It was something he didn't mention, not yet, not until he had enough time to know it was real, if some of his sight was dribbling back.

Trying to keep his voice even, even if his heart was beating like an Indian war drum, he said, dragging the words out of nowhere, "I'd take it kindly if you'd read me some of what you're writing."

Edwina didn't know what to do. With Tal sleeping most of

the time—except when she guided him outside to answer the calls of nature or he was eating—the lodge had been quiet. She had had time to finish one of the small books and start another. When they got back to Winnemucca, she intended to send these to her publishers, and fulfill that much of her contract. But she wasn't sure she wanted to read to Talmadge Jones—sinning in private was one thing, but exposing her sinful ways to him was something else.

"Mr. Jones, are you sure you want me to read . . . I mean, dime novels are rather silly."

"Silly maybe, but they aren't tools of the devil. Hell, kid, I was thinking I might do a little of that kind of writing to earn enough money to buy my beans and bacon. I heard somewhere that that writer Ned Buntline makes a pot of money. It seems to me that if a pie-headed idiot like that so-called gunslinger, Lobo Chance, can write books like that, then I damn sure could."

Edwina bent a little closer to the stack of papers in her lap, but she didn't tell Tal she was that pie-headed idiot, Lobo Chance. She couldn't start reading until she had swallowed the horde of inexplicable giggles that were dancing jigs in her throat. Giggles born of the knowledge that Talmadge Jones was going to accept her just as she was.

Or rather he was going to accept her with the sex change she had given herself. For one wild moment, her tongue came close to betraying her, almost formed the words, "There's one more thing you ought to know: I'm not a boy."

Chapter Seven

Clearing his throat, Ed started at the beginning. Tal closed his eyes and enjoyed the way the kid painted pictures with his husky voice and words. The writing was mature and better than Tal had expected, but there was room for improvement.

Listening closely, taking advantage of the easiness that was growing between them, Tal explained where the kid was making mistakes in several aspects of fastdraws, shooting, and horsemanship. The kid accepted the knowledge and used it, but he wasn't above arguing when he thought he was right and Tal was wrong.

The kid read for a long time. Tal appreciated every minute of the action-packed tale. When Ed got to the end of what he had written, Tal asked, "What's going to happen next? How are you going to get the hero out of the box canyon and through the tribe of Indians without killing him?" Tal couldn't see how it was going to be done—Ed had him stymied.

The kid laughed. It was a happy-sounding laugh that came close to being teasing, and he didn't answer Tal's questions.

"Well," she drawled, "I reckon you'll have to wait until I get it written to find out all that. Now, I'm going to get a drink of water, give you one and a little dose of laudanum, and set the beans to warming. Then I'm going to get some snow to melt for coffee water and go out to the stable to tend the horse."

After the kid left, Tal closed his eyes. After a few seconds, he opened them again to see if the faint light in the blackness of his vision was still there, or if he was doing a lot of wishful thinking. The pale light gave him hope that eventually his sight would return. At least enough of it so he could take the kid back to Winnemucca.

He pondered the possibilities as he drifted on the outer edges of sleep, hovering there until the kid was in the lodge. He was beholden to the kid, but it wasn't being beholden that was gnawing at him.

When Ed came back, Tal dropped into sleep, dreaming of things wonderful and proper with a woman. He awoke when the echoing reverberation of a single gunshot bored through the lodge walls. The noise broke the quiet into breath-holding listening and a tangle of whispered questions.

"What the hell? Who's doing the shooting?" Befuddled, Tal fought the darkness. He forgot, momentarily, that it was his own and tried to get up. He fell sideways, scrabbled around, sweeping his hands across the rough stone of the floor, searching for his boots and his Colts. He swore when he remembered his blindness and that the six-guns were gone.

"Is it rescuers, Mr. Jones? Or have the outlaws followed us here? Why are they shooting? I have to . . ." It sounded like the kid dropped whatever it was he was holding and ran outside.

"Kid, wait. Damn it all to hell, don't go tearing out there without taking the . . ." Tal's order came too late; even if he couldn't see, he knew the lodge was emptier by one before his orders were out of his mouth. The fool kid had gone rushing out to face the-devil-knows-what and was likely to get himself killed for his troubles if Tal didn't—

Didn't what?

What in the hell could he do? Talmadge Jones almost surrendered to despair, but there wasn't any quit in him. There had to be a way to do something and he intended to find it. *And do it.*

Edwina squinted as she left the lodge for the brighter light of the outdoors. It had stopped snowing, but the wind was still making its presence known, misting the tops of snowdrifts with blown snow, sculpting new shapes in the grotesque gallery. Edwina knew she should go back and get her coat, but first she had to discover what was happening.

She took several steps away from the lodge trying to see who had invaded her sanctuary, but the light was murky, giving the snow-covered landscape an eerie appearance. Pale bluish light reflected from snow-swathed hummocks and bushes. The cloud-ladened sky seemed to be within touching distance. Everything was white, bluish-white, or a pale shade of pewter.

Except for the two red mules she had cut loose from the wrecked buggy nearly two weeks before. They were flecks of distant color bucking and lunging in the deep snowdrifts clogging the mouth of the canyon, trying to escape from something or someone still not visible. Judging from the mules' frantic behavior, whatever was chasing them was getting closer.

Shivering and afraid, but knowing she had to discover who or what was invading the valley, Edwina pushed her way into the waist-high drift that fronted one side of the lodge entrance. Breaking through, she found easier walking on a thin layer of frozen snow. She had gone less than twenty feet when she stopped and peered intently, shading her eyes with her hand, trying to turn the blurs into something recognizable.

"Indians?" Staring through narrowed eyes, she shivered. What she feared was real. The Indians were at the mouth of the canyon. Easing back, Edwina scarcely took a breath until she was back inside the lodge and grabbing her coat. One of Tal's six-guns was in the pocket.

"Kid, what's going on out there? Who is it? What do they want?"

"Indians," she answered.

"Here?"

Edwina nodded before she remembered he couldn't see. "Yes. They're in the canyon. They're chasing the mules, or I think that's what they're doing. The mules were trying to get away and . . ."

One of Livy's fancy quilts was draped around him, hanging from his broad shoulders like a cape. Tal had found his boots and was standing with one hand holding onto the wall as he made his slow way toward the entrance.

"You said the skinner told you this place was abandoned after some of the tribal members died here, didn't you?"

"Yes, but . . ."

"Kid, if they are Paiutes, they won't come near this place. Their superstitions will keep them far away. You can bet on that."

Edwina took a single step toward the blanket-covered doorway before she paused and looked back. "And if they're not Paiutes, Mr. Jones?"

"I don't know what they'll do, but this is Paiute country. I'd guess it's a few of them hunting grub. Kid, you have to go out there and see what they're doing. Take the Winchester and . . ."

There was worry in his voice, but Edwina didn't know if it was for Ed's safety or for what the Indians might be planning. Her one word question didn't ease his concern. "Winchester?"

"The rifle?" He took in a quick breath and looked toward

her voice. "Oh, God, kid, you know how to shoot a gun, don't you?"

Did she? She knew how to quick-draw, she had practiced that in the attic back home, learning how to do it so she could describe it when writing about Lobo Chance. But as far as actual shooting went, she had never had occasion to pull a trigger. She equivocated. "I think I left the rifle in the buggy. I don't remember getting it out from under the seat. I have your revolver."

"Do you know how to shoot it?"

Edwina left the lodge without answering. She was sure she knew how to point the weapon, cock the hammer, and pull the trigger, but she didn't want to do any of it. She prayed the Indians would turn tail and run when they realized where they were. She feared they wouldn't. She knew if they came to kill there wasn't much she could do to stop them.

Was there?

Beginning to sweat, Edwina lifted the Colt from her pocket, pulled back the hammer with her thumb, and held the grip with a trembling hand. Blued-steel with a walnut handle, the Colt was heavy. She eased hand and gun down until both rested against her hip. Listening to the crunch of her own faltering steps in the snow, the cold keening of the wind, and the distance-softened guttural shouts of the Indians, Edwina tried not to think of the danger.

The wind nipped her face and crawled down her neck. She swallowed hard and kept walking. She had to cross the field of snow and discover what the Paiutes were doing. As she went, she prayed they were Paiutes and strong in their beliefs.

She would do whatever possible to save Tal and herself. Even if he was an outlaw, she couldn't let him die. "You're getting notional," she whispered. "That's what old maids do. Get notional and go dotty."

Whispering nonsense to herself to keep from turning and running, Edwina glanced back, endeavoring to erase the irrational fear that someone was sneaking up from behind her. She saw the steam rising from the hot springs, smoke drifting up out of the lodge smoke hole, but neither seemed threatening.

A gunshot froze her in place. It frightened her, but the Indians weren't shooting at her. All their attention was centered on the mules struggling to escape from the snowdrifts.

"Go on," she ordered her unwilling body She crouched low and sneaked from snow mound to wind-shaped bush. Her ally for the moment, the wind picked up speed and blew a haze of snow across the valley floor. It gave a hiding place as she crept close enough to see the seven Indian dressed in ragged garments of skins and faded cloth. One had a rifle and it was pointed at the mules.

Big Red and Rude were skinny. That didn't stop their fight to escape their pursuers.

Edwina edged closer to the drama that was unfolding in the mouth of the canyon. It was a mistake. Two of the Indians turned, saw her, and started shouting in a language she didn't understand. She was too terrified to do more than stand there, the cocked six-gun dangling from her shaking hand, and stare at what was surely her doom.

"Please, God, let it be quick," she whispered before she raised the Colt, intending to make them pay dearly for Tal's life and her own. He was helpless. She tried to stand straight and tall, but her knees were trembling badly, almost refusing to hold her weight.

"Stop it," she growled. Convinced she was going to her own execution, Edwina took another stumbling step forward.

The Indian raised the rifle. Probably the one she had left under the buggy seat, using this prod of guilt she moved toward the marauders. She needed to get closer if she intended the six-gun to inflict any damage.

The Indian fired. One of the mules screamed in agony, reared high, went down hard, and thrashed around in the snow. The other one, ears back, eyes wild, broke through the drift and bolted in Edwina's direction. He passed her at a dead run and kept right on going, heading up the valley as fast as he could travel.

The stricken mule screamed again. Its blood pulsed out, staining the snow. Kicking and jerking in its death throes, the animal screamed a final time.

The sounds high-pitched and charged with triumph, the Indians shouted. With a long-bladed knife held high, one advanced on the twitching mule. The others turned their attention to Edwina. Toting the rifle by the barrel, swinging it like a club, one man took the lead and moved toward her with slow deliberate steps. Edwina was too frightened to be the best judge, but she thought they were looking beyond her, staring at something back by the lodge.

They acted as if they were as scared as she was—which didn't seem possible.

The Indians stopped their advance, hesitated, and muttered among themselves. Shifting from foot to foot, they pointed toward the lodge and ignored her existence. Edwina saw how gaunt they were, how chilled and hungry-looking. Their faces, weren't painted. They just looked weary, cold, and frightened.

So much so that she felt a moment of compassion. The pity didn't stop her from extending her forefinger and snugging it around the icy trigger of the six-gun. Edwina used both hands to raise the Colt and point it toward the Indian with the rifle. She hoped she could see well enough to hit him in some vulnerable spot.

It was the time between daylight and night, but was neither. The snow was gray, the snow, the air, and even the wind held its own tinge of gray. The wind had grown stronger and was beginning to howl with a long, drawn-out, mournful sound. Ice crawling up her spine, Edwina shuddered. She almost screamed when she realized it wasn't the wind crying a heartbroken lament. Whoever or whatever was doing the wailing and weeping was coming up behind her.

Edwina's heart stopped, if only for a second. She held her breath until she thought her lungs would burst. Moving slowly and carefully, she turned her head and looked toward the lodge. Dry-mouthed, she stared at the figure making its way across the frozen waste.

Grave-cloths fluttering and flapping in the wind, a darker gray, ever-changing shape in a gray world, it was enough to frighten more than just the faint of heart. Faint of heart or not, she was too scared to move, or to shoot to save herself.

The specter from beyond its Indian grave, its arms held high, its mouth wide with the anguish of death, was staggering. Stumbling. Howling. Gibbering. Swaying. Dropping to its knees. Crawling. Moaning. And coming directly toward where she crouched.

She released one breath and gasped in another. Tal.

Most of Edwina's fear fled with the recognition. However, the Indians' fear was based on a lifetime of learning. They believed in ghosts of the dead who came back to claim new bodies; Tal's performance gave credence to their beliefs. Howling louder than the outlaw, they whirled and ran. Growing fainter with distance, their howls continued after they vanished into the canyon.

Tal crawled a foot or so farther, collapsed, and fell facedown in the snow. Breathing hard, he tried to howl but it sounded more like a groan. The wind lifted the quilt up and away from him. It flapped like the wings of a flightless bird.

Edwina released the hammer of the Colt and returned the weapon to her pocket. She stumbled to where the fallen gunfighter lay and said, "You can stop now. They're gone. You probably scared them into the next county—and me right along with them."

The kid sounded ready to spit fire, but Tal felt good that his plan had worked. He lay there, enjoying the feel of the cold beneath his cheek, and tried to hold back his laughter. It escaped, jumping out of his mouth and echoing in the air.

"Get up," the kid snapped. "Don't you have any sense at all? They could have killed you and . . . Stop laughing, damn it, and get up before you freeze to death."

Ed pulled at him, trying to get him to his feet. "Come on. Get up. It's getting dark. The Indians might come back and you . . ."

"They won't," he said, choking back the laughter that had gotten weaker and weaker. "They won't dare offend the *tum tum wawas.*"

The tugging stopped. The kid asked, his voice sounding scared, "Mr. Jones, are you raving again?"

"No, it's the spirit voices." He wanted to explain further, but the kid's renewed efforts brought Tal to his knees and then to his feet. His arm around the kid's shoulder, his legs unsteady, Tal let the kid lead him. He just did what Ed Parker said and kept walking.

"We're almost there." The boy panted for breath, but didn't release his hold on Tal's waist until they were inside the lodge. Resting on his pallet, Tal heard Ed fling a couple of heavy chunks of wood into the fire pit. He saw the ruddy glow of the fire as it flamed high. He started to tell Ed some of his sight might be coming back, but the kid stopped him with,

74

"The Indians looked so hungry and tired that I wanted to . . ."

There was nothing Tal could say to that. He asked, "Were they shooting at the mules? Is that why one of the animals was squealing?"

"It wasn't shot clean." The kid was moving around the fire pit nervously. Tal heard the coffee mill grinding, water being poured from one container to another, and more wood being added to the fire before the kid cleared his throat. "They'll come back, won't they? The Indians, I mean. To get the mule they killed? And in here to kill us so they can get what food we've got left?"

Tal knew they weren't real questions. At least, not ones he needed to answer, but he did anyway. "Yes, I guess they will, for the mule anyway. I doubt they'll come any further into the valley unless they're hungry enough to risk displeasing the spirits."

Chapter Eight

Gritting her teeth, Edwina tried to dislodge the fear that still clung to her. She stirred the fire. Sparks climbed upward with the smoke; the fire crackled and snarled. Nowhere in the valley was safe, the Indians were creeping closer and soon they would be bursting into the lodge, screaming and killing.

Edwina's fingers curled around the Colt in her right-hand coat pocket. Chills chased each other up her spine. Her voice was almost steady, and her breathing was only a little ragged when she asked, "Spirits? Here? What are you talking about? What are . . ."

"Ghosts," he answered. His voice sounded tired. "I don't know the Paiute language well, but in Chinook, the trade language, they call them *lejubes*. It means demons, ghosts, or spirits. Things you can't see, but are there, and most of the time, they aren't good. But they aren't bad exactly either; at least not in the way we mean when we say devils. The *tum tum wawas* are spirit voices, the voices of all things, living and dead. The voices you can almost hear in the wind and rain and late at night when . . ."

His teeth flashed white in the darkness of his whiskers. Edwina knew he was making light of something—maybe of his own half-belief that spirit voices existed. It was a spooky thought, but it didn't stop her from asking, "Will they keep the Indians out of here?"

"Kid, I don't know. I wish to God that I could tell you what's going to happen. I wish lots of things, but wishing doesn't change what is."

"What are we going to do?"

"Hope for the best. Get ready for the worst. Wait them out."

Punctuated by recurring snowstorms and the howling wind, the wait went on until it was almost a week in length. Beyond dragging away the dead mule the first night, the Indians made no further move. Neither did they go away.

Inside the lodge, life went on. She cooked. They ate. They spent most of their time conferring together, discussing the book they were working on together; the third one of the four she had promised Beadle and Adams. The days passed in seeming tranquillity, but it had an unreal aspect.

It wasn't as if she lived in constant fear, because she didn't. Or if she did, it was of something not even remotely connected to the lurking people in the canyon. The inspired was the title she chose for the book they were writing, presuming they lived to finish it and *Lurkers in the Canyon* was published.

She was beginning to have feelings for Tal. Her awareness of him grew more acute when he refused to take any more of the laudanum. He insisted on being led around, with his arm around her shoulders, to regain his strength.

She found it difficult to breathe when she sneaked out at dawn and dusk to spy on the Indians. The starving mule returned and allowed her to shoo him into the stable with the horse.

Her hopes for the Indians' rapid departure were unrealized. She searched for new ways to busy herself and new words to tell herself she was being foolish. Even if he wasn't one of the outlaws who had abducted her sister, Talmadge Jones was still a gunfighter. Blind, but dangerous. Unshaven and bandaged, handsomer than any man she had ever seen, he would not want to be saddled with a vinegar-tongued old maid.

"I think my sight might be coming back a little," he said on the morning of the seventh day after he had frightened the Paiutes. "I can see light and shadows, and maybe even tell when it's pitch dark."

Edwina didn't try to hide her joy. "Oh, Mr. Jones, that's truly wonderful. I read, in one of the newspapers back home, about a doctor in San Francisco who has done wonders with restoring sight. Maybe we could . . ." Suddenly aware her tongue was betraying her, Edwina gulped and swallowed. "Maybe *you* could go to California and have him . . ."

It was too late.

"Kid," Tal said, hunching closer to the fire, "don't take me wrong, but, much as I'd admire to have you beside me, it's not going to happen. I've been a loner for too long. It's no kind of life for a kid like you, one with a family and a future. Besides, after we find your sister and those two girls of hers, they're going to need you. Judging from what I know of Raiter, that family of his is going to need you more than you know."

A gust of wind rattled the lodge, came down the smoke hole, swirled smoke and sand into their faces. It saved Edwina by turning her sob into a cough. "I imagine you're right about the needing, not that Livy will allow me to help. I left enough money in the bank back home to see Mother and my aunt through six months or longer, so if we can just get this third book finished, then I'll have some money to—to help Livy if she . . ."

Shivering more with a sense of doom than with actual cold, she rubbed her hands together, trying to warm them and to drive out the *lejubes* that seemed intent on destroying what little peace of mind she had left. Edwina sighed and buried her face in her icy hands. She didn't tell Tal her secret fear that Livy was walking straight toward her own death. Sooner or later, Ambrose would beat her until her life was gone and . . .

"The girls," she whispered, intent on the horror she saw in her own mind and unaware she was speaking aloud. "Dear God, what will happen to the girls? He's their father, but I can't let Ambrose . . ."

"Kid," Tal said, getting to his feet and feeling his way around the curve of the wall "don't let it get to you. We'll get out of here. If the Paiutes haven't come in here by now, then I'm guessing they won't come at all. They'll hightail it out as soon as the weather clears, and we'll be right behind them."

She knew he was trying to comfort her. "It'd better be soon. We've used most of the wood that was stored in here and the horse and the mule are eating themselves out of hay." She said it like a boy giving a report to an older man. One that he respected, admired, and, God help her, was beginning to trust.

Tal was close enough to touch Edwina on the shoulder. "How about our own food supply, kid? Seems like we've been eating a fair amount ourselves, so how's it lasting?"

That simple question added a new dimension to her concern. There was enough food, if they left soon. It wasn't the food that was the worry. It was how they were going to transport it since she had wrecked the buggy.

As if he could read her mind, Tal reached out, brushed the side of her face with his hand before it settled on her shoulder and gave it a man-to-boy squeeze. "Did you bring my saddle when you took off?"

Tal was no longer helpless. Blind or not, he was a man and

he was standing too close. She wanted to move, step away from him, and release the breath that was caught in her throat. Perhaps it was the lack of air that caused her answer to come out in a squeak "Yes."

"We'll do fine, kid. I reckon that mule you saved hasn't been broken to ride, but from the feel of you, you don't weigh much. The gelding won't balk at carrying double until we can get another horse."

"A horse?"

He chuckled. "What's the matter, Ed? You know how to ride a horse, don't you?"

Ride a horse? Edwina could drive a team of mules across the high desert in the middle of winter, but not once in her life had she been on the back of a horse. Lifting her chin, Edwina looked at him squarely, glad for the moment that his blind eyes could not see the flush of guilt that dyed her face. "Yes," she said, forcing surliness into her voice, "of course, I can ride."

Tal accepted the lie, but he knew it for what it was. Tenderfoot or not, the kid had grit—and grit was what it was going to take to get them somewhere safe. The kid's grit and his own savvy might be enough to . . .

"OK," he said, grinning at the shadow person that stood between him and the fire, "now that we've got that settled, what about the grub? It'll take us a week or longer to get to Winnemucca. Do we have enough food for that?"

The kid stepped away from Tal's hand on his shoulder. "If the Indians leave soon and we leave not too long after, then we shouldn't have any problem."

He felt his way back to his bedroll. He sat down on the end of it and said, his confession hesitant, "Kid, I haven't been totally honest with you. I don't know who did the killing and stealing. But you ought to know that Raiter hired me to meet the wagons near the border between Nevada and Oregon and see that they got to his saloon. He didn't say a word about his family being on the train; he just wanted his whiskey brought in safe."

"Why?" the kid asked. "Why would you work for a man like that?"

He hadn't the words to explain the years of emptiness, the coldness that was destroying him, or his need to get warm.

Instead, he said, "I needed the money. Kid, I'm not a hero from one of those little books we're writing. I'm a gunfighter and I fight for whoever pays me. Ambrose Raiter was paying me to protect his property and to do any killing that had to be done."

Looking straight ahead, he allowed the grimness inside him to spill over into his words. "When I caught up with the wagon train, that's what I intended doing. Killing anybody dumb enough to try and steal the whiskey, even when I knew Raiter was probably going to sell some of it to the Indians and get a whole lot more settlers burned out or killed. That doesn't make me any better than Raiter."

Silence followed. Tal couldn't see the kid, but he could hear him breathing and making gulping sounds.

"Mr. Jones," the kid said, his voice quieter and huskier than usual, but steady, "thank you for telling me. I appreciate it."

"Kid, I . . ."

"The storm's over," Ed said, "and it's getting on toward night. I'd better take care of the animals." The kid was gone before Tal could stop him. The fire had died to pale embers when the kid came back. "I think the Indians left." He sounded as subdued as Tal felt, but he said nothing about Tal's confession. He didn't speak more as he added wood to the fire, built it up to a brisk flame, and started grinding coffee.

Tal waited several minutes. "That's good. Give them a day or two, and then, if the weather holds, we can load up and . . ." The words died in his throat. He wanted to bring back the ease to their relationship but didn't know how.

The kid surprised him. After they had eaten another bait of beans and hoe cake, Ed said, "*Lurkers in the Canyon* is almost half finished. Mr. Jones, do you think we could work on it some more tonight? I'd like to have as much written as possible before we have to leave."

Smiling foolishly, Tal swallowed hard before he could say, "Sounds good to me, kid. That is, if you really want me to."

"Well, of course I do, Mr. Jones.

The sun was coming up when Edwina held the gelding while Tal crawled into the saddle. His every move made her realize just how much they were leaving behind in the canyon. Not their worldly goods, although they had left some of those, but the closeness they had shared.

"Ready, kid?" Tal asked, pulling at the quilt she had fashioned into a hooded wrap and tied around him.

"Ready." Placing the loaded mule's lead rope in Tal's hand, Edwina grabbed the horse's reins and took the first step of what looked to be a terrible journey. One that was going to be even worse when they got out of the canyon and were forced to ride double.

The thought gave her the shivers. By the time she had broken through snowdrifts, stumbled across hidden boulders, sweated a pint or two, and walked the full length of the canyon, she was too tired to shiver. Or to worry about what would happen when Talmadge Jones discovered that she wasn't a boy.

Taking a deep breath, blowing it out with more force than necessary, knowing she couldn't delay the moment of truth any longer, Edwina broke through the final drift. She stepped out of the canyon into the sun-glittered world of the snowy high desert, stopped short, stared with unbelieving eyes, and whimpered deep in her throat.

"What is it?" Tal asked. "What's wrong?"

Edwina couldn't answer or stop staring.

"Damn it, kid, tell me what's wrong."

"We're lost," she whispered. "There's no trail or anything."

Chapter Nine

Tal took a deep breath of icy air. He was going to have to add new worries to those Ed was carrying, and was not something he wanted to do. It should have been done before they left the canyon, but he had kept hoping that his sight would return and he could provide the necessary protection.

Squinting, Tal tried to force his eyes to see something, anything that would enable him to tell the kid things were going to be all right. It wasn't possible. He could see light, lots of it, enough to make his eyes tear up but not much else.

"Lost," the kid whispered again. "Mr. Jones, we . . . This has to be the way we went into the canyon, but it doesn't look like anyplace I've seen."

Tal shifted in the saddle, rubbed his fingers down his frosty mustache and plotted their next move. Ed was tired and a tenderfoot, a fuzzy-faced kid shouldering more worries and responsibilities that anyone should.

With his sister and her girls being taken and Ed having to take care of a blind man, it was possible that being lost out in the sand and sage was the last straw. Still, it wasn't time to pitch in his hand and call it quits.

"It was the storm, I guess," he said, trying to rip through the haze that clouded his memory. His fingers moved up to touch the tender scar on his forehead. "If I remember correctly, just before I rode into the freighters' camp, there was a big storm building. It probably covered our tracks with sand or scoured them off the face of the earth. We can still find our way out. All we have to do is head east and south until we find the main trail coming north from Winnemucca."

Tal waited for the kid to say something.

"Mr. Jones," the kid said, coming to stand beside the horse, "is something wrong? Does your head hurt?"

"No," he said, sounding sharper than he intended. "Nothing's wrong, but there's a hell of lot that could be, if we don't do something about it now."

Hoisting himself out of the saddle, he dismounted and tried to find the words that wouldn't destroy what small trust the boy had given him. "Where are my belts and guns?"

He heard the crunch of frozen snow as the kid backed away, heard the coldness that crept into Ed's husky voice. "Why?"

"Because . . ." Releasing his grip on the saddle, he took a single step toward the sound. Stumbled, flailed his arms. Tal managed to regain his balance, but he felt an odd sense of loneliness when the kid didn't rush to his aid.

"I have one of the guns in my pocket. The other one and your gun belts are in the pack on the mule."

The kid sounded as if every scrap of suspicion he'd had of Tal was back and growing. Tal couldn't let that stop him. He'd sworn, by whatever honor he had left, to get the kid someplace safe so he could find out what had happened to his sister, and that's just what was going to happen. Taking in a breath, willing his voice to be soft, Tal ordered, "Get them."

"Why?"

Tal snapped, "We need 'em, that's why."

Before Edwina could question the order, he added, "Kid, don't fight me on this. It has to be done right now."

Edwina didn't understand, but she knew she wasn't going

to give him the guns unless he explained further. In the canyon, except for a few little nagging doubts, she had believed him when he said he wasn't with the outlaws. Maybe she still more than half believed he was innocent, but she couldn't take the chance.

She shook her head and tried not to look at him. He was standing there with the bright sunlight curling around him, making him a part of the light. The canyon's dark mouth loomed behind him. Tal stood tall, legs wide, practically glaring at her, demanding a trust she wasn't yet ready to give. Wrapped in the rainbow colors of Olivia's wedding-ring quilt, swaying like a willow in the wind, he should have looked absurd, pitiful.

But he didn't. Dignity enveloped him, took away the dirt and pain, made her see just what he was. Fierce and proud as a wounded eagle and so terribly vulnerable that she ached to give him what he wanted.

Pushing her own feelings aside, Edwina lifted her chin, took a quick breath, and repeated her earlier question "Why do you want them?"

"Ed," he said quietly, "I know you don't have any reason to trust me, but will you at least listen?"

She nodded, then remembered he couldn't see. "Yes."

"Things were different in the canyon. But there are dangers in the high desert that . . . Kid, tell me the honest-to-God truth, have you ever shot a six-gun in your life?"

Remembering the many hours spent in the attic practicing the fast draw with her grandfather's dueling pistol, Edwina told the truth—if not all of it. "No," she said softly. "No, Mr. Jones, I never have."

If Olivia didn't tell the world about the sinful writing, there was still the fact that Edwina Parkhurst, spinster, had spent many nights alone with a man. Tongues would wag.

She could see the hurt and shame in her mother's eyes as the preacher denounced her and cast her out of the congregation.

He interrupted her dark thoughts. "If we're going to make it to Winnemucca, Ed, you have to learn how to shoot and to kill if you have to."

Pushing her way through the drifts in the canyon had been hard enough to make her sweat. She wasn't warm now. She was cold to her bones and it wasn't the weather that was turning her to ice. There were murderous outlaws and starving savages roaming around. They were dangerous and she was all the protection . . .

Jones took her thought to its conclusion. "We both need a gun, Ed. You knowing how to shoot will help, but if anything happens to you . . ." He gave his head a slight shake, gnawed at his bottom lip, and continued, "I hate the cold, kid. I need one of those guns. If anything happens and I'm out here alone, I don't want to freeze to death."

Her throat was too tight for speech. Edwina swallowed, then swallowed again, but she knew better than to offer false reassurance. Tal had offered her the truth; she would honor it.

"I'll get the other gun and the belts."

"The cartridges, too. There should have been a couple of boxes in my bedroll."

She did as he asked.

Tal heard Ed slide the six-shooter into the oiled leather of the holster before the kid said, "I don't know which way is south."

Tal could smell the horse. He moved in its direction and swung himself up. He eased back until he was sitting behind the saddle. "Well, that's easy. Where's the sun?"

"Almost straight up. Our shadows are right under our feet. There are clouds building up, too. I don't think the sun's going to be shining much longer."

This was going to take some thinking. Tal scratched at his beard. "Mount up. Give the horse his head. He's smart. Maybe he knows the way back to the main trail. If he doesn't, then maybe he'll take us to a landmark you remember."

"Yes, sir," Ed said. His voice was low, but Tal detected more fear in it than before. He was feeling apprehensive himself and was worried about what was going to happen.

Edwina clung to the saddle horn with both hands. She tried to breath and to still her panic. She felt like she was on top of a mountain. She was going to fall, she knew it.

"Relax," Tal said, his warm breath coming in under her hat to touch her ear. It wasn't until her teeth started chattering from the cold that he enveloped her in his quilt, pulled her back against him, and held her securely with one arm around her waist.

"I guess it'll take a little while for you to get used to riding again," he said, sounding too serious to be believed.

Edwina sighed and confessed another of her falsehoods. "I've never ridden a horse. Horses aren't . . ." She stopped her wayward tongue before it could say, "Riding astride a horse isn't considered the proper mode of transport for ladies."

He chuckled. "I figured that. You'll get the hang of it quickly, but you're going to be almighty sore in the morning."

She wasn't worried about being sore. Edwina was worried that his hands might move up, feel the swell of her small bosom, discover exactly what she was. Discover Ed Parker, the boy who had taken care of him in all ways possible, was a woman.

She drew in a sharp breath. She might be a sinner, but she

wasn't a wanton. She needed the physical warmth his body was giving hers to survive the cold, but she would keep her secret until they were safe.

They paused once to rest the horse. Edwina thought it was about mid-afternoon, but she had no way of knowing for sure. Clouds, gray and chilly, had pushed their way across the sky until there wasn't a hint of sunlight. The landscape wore the same dull color. Even the alkali pans and the snow drifts looked soiled. The eternal wind whined a lament that was in keeping with the scene.

While the horse rested, Edwina practiced with the revolver. Drawing and aiming, just to get the feel of the weapon, to know its weight and her own strength. She didn't think about killing. She hoped she would do what had to be done and worry about the consequences later.

Listening to the hiss of metal sliding out of leather, Tal tried to gauge how well the boy was doing. His draw sounded smooth, almost too smooth, as if he had practiced it before. "Remember," he said, "fast isn't what counts. You've got to aim true and squeeze the trigger. Kid, I'm not sure anything will happen. I'm not betting on anything."

"Do you . . . uh . . . do you think she's . . ."

He wanted to give the kid comfort and tell him his sister and nieces were alive, but he couldn't. This was a harsh land, and some of the men who traveled through it were uncivilized. He wouldn't be doing the kid any favors by holding out false hope. "I wish I knew," was all he said before he changed the subject to add, "The horse has had enough rest. We'd better ride out."

When they were mounted, Tal said, "It gets dark early. Keep your eye out for a sheltered spot to spend the night. There should be a hot spring around somewhere—the country is riddled with them. If you find one, take a good look before you let the animals drink."

"Why? Do you think Indians might . . ."

"No. It's just that some of the springs have so much alkali in them that they're poisonous. Look for tracks. If rabbits and other animals come to drink, then it'll be okay for us to use."

She could barely walk when she dismounted inside the small grove of junipers she had chosen for their camp. The trees surrounded a rocky declivity that held a pool of water in its lower end. It had animal trails all around it. The wind rustled the branches, but inside the shelter it felt warm in comparison to the cold they had been traveling through. It grew warmer still after Edwina hobbled around, settled the horse and mule for the night, and gathered enough dry sage to build a pungent, crackling fire.

In short order, she had the packs open, the bedrolls spread, the coffeepot emitting a plume of steam, and ham sizzling in the iron frying pan. Sitting close to the warmth of the fire, Tal asked, "Ed, if you had the money and could go anywhere in the world, where would you go?"

It wasn't something she had thought about, except in guilty, stolen moments. She had had no clear idea about where she would go. "I don't know," she said finally, turning the ham so it would brown on the other side. "Where would you go, Mr. Jones?"

"Tal," he snapped. "Call me Tal. When you say Mr. Jones like that, it makes me sound old enough to be your father."

Edwina laughed.

Sounding irritable, he said, "I suppose I *am* old enough to be your father."

A stick snapped in the fire, sending up a shower of sparks. A coyote howled in the distance. Edwina bit her bottom lip to keep from laughing again, but was unable to keep every hint of merriment out of her voice when she said, "Mr. Jones, I mean, Tal, I may not be as young as you think. Or maybe you're a lot older than you look."

He made a noise that wasn't quite a word.

Edwina speared the ham with her knife, jerked it onto a tin plate, and poured coffee in the frying pan to make a sop to heat up the pan bread she had saved from their morning meal. When it was ready, she placed his plate in his hands. Not wanting to call forth more protest from her abused body, she stood to eat her own supper.

Coyotes yipped and howled, sounding much closer, making her too aware of the vastness of the unpeopled space all around them. She drew in a shuddery breath and bent to toss more brush onto the coals. The heat didn't reach very far, but the dance of light gave her a small measure of reassurance. Or it would have if Tal hadn't said, "Better not build the fire too high. You can see a long way out here. I don't think we want to lead any strangers to our camp."

The next bite of ham stuck in her throat. She swallowed hard, felt the pain as it went down, and asked the question she had been dreading "What about tonight? Will we need to stand watch or . . ."

"I don't know, kid. We both need the sleep, but . . ."

The firelight touched his face with glancing fingers, revealing nothing. He sat there for a minute or two before he grinned, his teeth flashing bright in the chancy light, and said, "I guess we'll be safe enough for now."

Weariness and a longing to be held and comforted like a tired child washed over her. It took away most of her common sense and she came perilously near to blurting out her secret. She managed to hold that back, but her wagging tongue seemed to have developed a mind of its own. Her other secrets were sent flying into the Nevada night.

"Why is that, Mr. Jones? Are your *tum tum wawas* going to warn us if there's danger?"

Tal knew the kid was scared. He could hear the fear in Ed's voice, but the tartness surprised him as much as the question.

"Well, as to that, I couldn't say, but, kid, it's cold enough to freeze the devil's hind leg off, so he won't be out here looking for us. As far as the savages go, they've got enough sense to hole up in this kind of weather."

"What about the outlaws?"

He tried to think of something that would ease the kid's fear. "Look, kid, forget about the outlaws for a minute," he said finally. "Instead of them, think about that pie-head, Lobo Chance. Think what he would do. Would he be scared out of his leather britches, jumping and sweating every time the wind rattled the brush? Or would he just crawl in his bedroll, warm his bones, and sleep the night away like he was resting in the finest hotel in San Francisco?"

"He wouldn't be doing any of those things," the kid said, sounding like he was either about to bawl or laugh. It was hard to tell which, so Tal figured he'd better step pretty light and keep his mouth shut until the kid had a chance to cool off.

It wasn't until the kid started to clean their plates that Tal asked the question that had been bothering him. "How do you know what Lobo Chance would do, kid? Is he a friend of yours?"

"Lobo Chance is a hero. He saves damsels in distress, shoots all the villains, and rescues the innocent and lost. He doesn't have any friends," Ed said.

"I suppose he killed them all," Tal growled. "Or maybe he just talked them all to death telling those bragging tales of his deeds."

Ed's chuckle was soft, low, and infuriating. It poked at

what might have been a bit of jealousy lurking in the darker places of Tal's mind. It goaded him into saying, "Well, if he's so great, I suppose you wish he was here now so he could save our miserable hides."

The kid laughed again. It didn't have a happy ring to it. He sounded sad when he answered, "He is, Mr. Jones. Lobo Chance is right here. And he doesn't know any more about saving us than I do."

Chapter Ten

The fire had died down. The heat still burned his face, but Tal could see well enough to know the blaze was a different color, redder, more like hot coals than the orange of leaping flame. He could hear the gelding and mule moving around, grazing on rabbit brush. It was a familiar sound, one that didn't hint at danger, but the boy's words were sending little chills racing up his spine.

"Kid," Tal asked, pondering what Ed had said in disbelief, "are you trying to tell me you're Lobo Chance?"

"Yes."

The kid's voice was flat, but daring Tal to dispute his claim. Tal didn't. He couldn't figure out what was going on.

It wasn't the first time Ed had lied, but those other lies were kid talk. They were a fuzzy-faced boy trying to make himself out to be older and bigger than he really was by saying he could ride and shoot. But Ed claiming to be Lobo Chance didn't make any sense.

"I am Lobo Chance," the kid said. His voice was raised.

No matter what Ed claimed, it wasn't possible. Lobo Chance's tall tales had been around for years, Tal was sure of that. He could remember reading one in Santa Fe and he hadn't been there since the summer of '68. If what Ed was saying was true, it would make the kid a lot older than he acted or sounded.

Tal sucked in a breath, pulled the quilt a little tighter around himself. "Ed, you don't have to . . . Well, it's all right with me if you're . . ."

He wanted to tell Ed Parker that he was tops in Tal's book. There wasn't any need for him to be claiming to be what he wasn't. Tal sighed, shifted his body, trying to find a softer spot on the rock beneath him.

"Look," he said finally, picking over his words carefully. He didn't want to rile the kid, but he didn't want Ed to think he was swallowing the tale either. "We've come a long way today. My bones are hurting and more than likely yours are too, so why don't we just crawl into our bedrolls and do our talking about this when . . ."

The kid didn't respond.

"Oh, hell," Tal said finally. "It doesn't make any difference to me, kid. If you want to . . ." Another thought nudged at the edges of his mind, a sly thought that had more to do with the way he was feeling about the boy than what was the truth. What if there was still more lies? What if the kid was older and *maybe not a boy?*

Tal caught his breath and allowed the thought to linger for a second. "It's the cold," he muttered. "The cold is . . ."

There was a slight sound, one out of the ordinary. He wasn't sure what it was or where it was coming from, but it was enough to tense his body. "Kid," he whispered, "there's something out there. You got your six-gun handy?"

Ed might be a liar, but he had grit. There wasn't a hint of fear in his husky voice when he said, "Yes, sir," and eased over to stand beside Tal who had risen to a crouch and was holding his own gun. "The fire's still pretty bright. Should we move away from it so . . ."

About then, Tal heard the click of a hoof on stone and knew what the invader was. "Antelope," he said, sitting back down. "Coming in to water. Throw some more brush on the fire real easy. Maybe you can see them."

"What about outlaws or—"

"Antelopes are the spookiest critters on the face of God's earth likely they've been watching us a spell, long enough to know we mean them no harm. So, I don't imagine there's anything else out there."

Returning the pistol to the holster riding low on her hip, Edwina took a deep breath. She held it for a long moment, expelled it, and took in another while she willed her heart to slow and the fear to dissipate. Even after doing that, she couldn't keep her hands from shaking as she slid some dry sagebrush onto the coals. Squinting at the burst of light, she moved away from the heat and shaded her eyes to peer down toward the small pond of water.

Turned a shimmering coral by the firelight, steam lifting from the surface of the hot spring curled upward and drifted in abstract swirls of light and shadow. It veiled the three drinking antelopes and turned the shy, graceful creatures into ghosts, things barely seen and impossibly beautiful. They came out of the black night, drank, then between one heartbeat and the next they lifted their heads, wheeled with dainty precision, and were gone, vanished as if they had never been.

"Oh," Edwina whispered, the sound scarcely more than an exhaled breath but fully expressing her sense of loss. Tears blurred her sight—not entirely for the beauty of the antelope, but for what their innocence and grace had forced to the forefront of her thoughts: her missing nieces, girls just as shy, graceful, and innocent as the thirsty beasts.

With the hurt came a fury so unexpected that it shook her and almost made her physically ill. "Why?" she whispered, her voice trembling. "Olivia, you're their mother. Why did you bring them here? Why did you do this to them?" She wasn't aware that she was speaking aloud until Tal said, "Kid? What's the matter?" He got to his feet and took a single step toward her.

Wanting to lean on his strength, but refusing to allow herself that small weakness, Edwina backed away. She couldn't stop the words spilling from her mouth. "She didn't have to come out here."

"Who?"

"My sister. Olivia Raiter. I offered to pay for the divorce. But, no, she wouldn't do that. Divorce is a terrible sin. My sweet sister doesn't sin. No, she had to obey that damned preacher, do her wifely duty, and come out here . . . come out here to—to . . . I hope the outlaws shot her."

"Kid? What are you saying?" Tal stumbled as he took another step toward her, went down on one knee, swore, struggled to regain his footing. "Kid, stop that fool talk and—"

"And what, Mr. Jones?" Edwina didn't wait for him to answer. "You know what Ambrose Raiter's like. If this hadn't happened, if we had gone on to his place, he would have killed her anyway. Sooner or later. And he wouldn't have done it easy. He likes to hurt."

"Ed?" Tal took a hesitant step forward, moving toward where he thought Edwina was standing. The quilt draped around his shoulders was dragging on the ground. Shadows hovered behind him, but the firelight flickering across his bearded face revealed the full measure of his concern.

"Don't worry, Mr. Jones. I only meant Olivia would be better off if the outlaws shoot her than if we find someone to rescue her. Sooner or later, Ambrose will beat her to death anyway, and when she's gone, the girls will . . . He's a vicious beast, but he won't kill them, will he? No, he'll just—just—

just sell . . ." The knowledge was sicken, but she knew, as plainly as if it were already a fact, what her brother-in-law would do to his daughters.

The fire crackled and snapped. Sparks shot up. They glittered in the frosty air like small orange stars. The omnipresent wind cried. Except for an occasional movement, the mule and horse were quiet.

Tal and Edwina were equally silent until she walked back to stand by the fire. She stared into the flames a moment. "My mother wanted to keep the girls. She asked Olivia to allow them to stay with her until Olivia got settled at Ambrose's homestead. But Olivia ran to the church to ask what was right and proper. The preacher said children belong with their parents, just like a wife belongs to her husband."

"Ed, I—"

She ignored him. "It isn't right. Men like Ambrose can beat their wives, abandon them in strange cities with no food and no money, and then, years later, demand they come running."

Memories came to Edwina of Olivia's battered face, the thin children, the fear in all their eyes when she had gone to Philadelphia in answer to Olivia's plea for aid after Ambrose had left her and the girls destitute. If Livy and the girls were still alive and if they could be rescued from the outlaws, it would happen again. It or something far worse. Ambrose Raiter would still be the same vicious animal he had always been. She sighed, adding the small sound to the wind's mourning dirge.

"Ed," Tal said, hunching down under the quilt. "I don't have any answers to give you. It's the way it's always been. Women are weak. They can't get along without a man to—"

"Only because men have made them believe that hog wash and have made sure they don't have any opportunity to find out the truth." She stopped, swallowed hard and dug her fingernails into the palms of her hands. "Mr. Lincoln didn't really free all the slaves, did he?" she asked, not trying to temper the bitterness that flooded the words.

"I reckon not," he answered, not like he was agreeing but more like he was thinking about it. "No, I reckon after all is said and done, he didn't."

After Edwina was in her bedroll, hurting in every part of her, she tried to stifle the sense of foreboding the open desert gave her. The Indian lodge had had walls to keep out the night. Here there was nothing but the waste, the wind, and the coyotes. She spent a long, restless night, one troubled with dark dreams that fled with the coming of the gray dawn.

The new day set the pace for the three that followed: practicing with the silent six-gun, loading the mule, mounting up, and allowing the gelding to have his head as he plodded along under an overcast sky. Edwina searched the bleak landscape for a landmark to guide them.

Lobo Chance hadn't been mentioned by either of them again.

About mid-afternoon of the third day of their journey, the gelding stopped.

"Mr. Jones?"

The kid's voice penetrated Tal's cold-induced daze. He opened his eyes, lifted his head, and looked around. He couldn't see much except a sort of mottled grayness. For a minute, he thought his sight, which had gotten slightly better each passing day, had gone bad again. He took a breath of icy air.

"It's not time to camp for the night, but it's getting really foggy."

Earlier, after they had stopped to eat a few bites, rest the horse, and attend to the calls of nature, the kid had fastened another thick quilt around Tal's shoulders and draped it over their front, giving their legs an extra layer of warmth against the cold. It hadn't added much to Tal's comfort. He was cold, frozen right down to the bone, and the kid's announcement made him colder. Fog on the high desert was bad, but fog when it was this cold could be . . .

It wasn't a question he wanted to ask. Dreading the answer, he swiped his frosty mustache and asked, "What does it look like?"

"Like the fog is frozen. It glitters like little bits of glass. I think it's getting thicker. It's really hard to see more than twenty feet."

It wasn't the answer he wanted to hear. Swallowing back a string of curses, Tal said, *"Pogonip,"* making the Paiute name for a killer fog sound like a knell of doom. If they weren't lucky, that's just what it could be.

"What?"

"Ed, find us a camping place real quick. We have to have shelter or . . ." The gelding began moving. The lead rope for the mule jerked at Tal's hand, but the mule followed quietly enough after only a brief foray into mulish rebellion. He said again, "Hurry, kid. We won't have much time to set up camp."

"Why?"

"A killer fog. *Pogonip.* It freezes on . . ." The kid turned his upper body slightly. His breath was warm on Tal's icy face. Tal's chilled brain wanted to draw conclusions that were wishes more than fact. The kid wasn't a woman, was he? The niggling suspicion had been steadily growing.

Ed twisted her body until she was almost facing Tal. She asked again, her voice rising a little, "What is it? Mr. Jones, what's the matter?"

"The fog. It freezes on everything it touches and it gets cold. A hell of lot colder than it is now. We have to get somewhere that gives us a little shelter. If we can't keep warm, we'll be . . ."

The kid turned away and spoke to the gelding, urging him to a faster pace. Grateful for the meager warmth and trying to sort out troubled thoughts, Tal huddled close against the boy's back. He knew what *Pogonip* could do and wanted to protect the kid.

Sucking in a breath, he said, "Find a canyon or something, kid, so the animals can have some shelter, too. And wood, we'll need lots of wood. It's going to get a hell of lot colder before it gets any warmer."

Tal was scared right down to his icy-cold toes. If he couldn't trust himself in this, they were in for a bad time. The kid had saved his miserable hide and had kept them both warm and fed.

He wasn't a simpering miss, Ed. As cold as they were, his lips twitched, wanted to smile, a patch of warmth that felt suspiciously like laughter spread in his belly. Whoever or whatever else the kid was or wasn't, Tal finally believed he had told the exact truth about one thing: Ed Parker was Lobo Chance. That meant, if his figuring was correct, he wasn't a child or even a young boy. He was old enough to be a man— and that seemed unlikely. His chaotic thoughts rambled on, coming up with wild hypotheses, and taking them as truth until he reached the inevitable conclusions—Ed was a woman.

Even if it was true, and Tal wasn't certain in spite of the logical sequence of his deductions, Ed was not a woman to be loved and courted by the likes of Talmadge Jones. He knew that, and if he couldn't do anything else, he would make real sure he didn't do anything to hurt her.

Ed reined in the gelding. "I can't see it very well, but there's a ravine here. It looks kind of deep and there's sort of a trail, but it's really steep. I'm going to have to lead the animals down."

Wiggling free from the quilts, the kid slid out of the saddle and dismounted before Tal could protest. But he did manage to corral his scattered senses enough to say, "Don't get out of sight. If we get separated, we—"

"I won't, but maybe you'd better get in the saddle and hang on."

He did that and was thankful. The kid was telling the truth when he said it was steep. Nearly freezing without the boy's warmth in front of him, Tal gripped the saddle horn with both hands. It wasn't a long ride, but it seemed to be, especially since all he could see was a light-flecked wall of gray.

"Easy, boy," Ed said softly, as the horse lurched and hopped sideways, amidst a clatter of falling rock. "Come on," he crooned. His voice was mild and coaxing, but Tal thought he could hear a note of panic in it. "There now," Ed said, relieved, "we're down."

The mule, despite the tether Tal still gripped in his icy hand, scrambled past the horse with a heavy clatter of shod hooves on stone. The rope jerked, slid through Tal's fingers, and was lost. He swore, and his thunderous words echoed in the narrow space Ed had found for their shelter. "The blasted mule," Tal bellowed. "He's loose. Dammit all to hell, I—"

"No," Ed said. "It's all right. He just wanted to get down. I have him."

Tal started to dismount.

Evidently Ed could see farther than Tal thought because he stopped him. "Wait. It's sort of dark down here, but not as cold as it was out in the open. It looks like . . . Could there have been a flood here or something like that?"

"Yeah. When it rains in the mountains, these little canyons are death traps. Flash floods roar down, destroying everything in their paths."

"Well," she said, after a brief pause. "I don't imagine we're in much danger of that happening now, are we?"

"Not when it's this cold."

"Good, there's some wood, piled up like a flood left it. Wait there. I'm going to tie up the mule and start a fire."

Tal fought against the shivery shakes that were beginning to crawl up him. "I hate this. If we ever get out of this godforsaken desert, I'm going someplace warm. Someplace where the sun shines twenty-four hours a day. And I'm going to stay there the rest of my life."

He thought Ed laughed, but it was hard to tell what with the other noises. From the sounds, he guessed Ed was dragging wood around and unloading the mule. He could do nothing but wait, muttering against the cold like an old, used-up gunfighter.

Even if the kid was a woman, she deserved a hell of lot more than he could give her. Hell, while he was being honest, he had to admit he couldn't give her a damn thing. He couldn't even look at her square and tell her she was beautiful. He was trying to build a truth on the odor of violets and his own wild suspicions, and he knew it. Tal winced at the memory of certain functions the kid had performed for him during his recovery. Ed sure wasn't a squeamish woman!

Swiping the lucifer along the sandpaper strip, praying the match would light, Edwina huddled over the tiny heap of grass, twigs, and sagebrush and tried for the fourth time to set it ablaze. The sulfur match sputtered once, went out. Fingers shaking with cold, she tried again. She was too cold to take even a measure of satisfaction when the grass smoldered fitfully and then brightened into a small, rapidly spreading flame.

Waiting until it was truly burning, Edwina added larger wood before beginning her other chores. The mule was unloaded, covered with a quilt, and tied securely before she threw down a ground cloth, tossed their bedrolls on top, and returned to Talmadge Jones and the horse.

It was still daylight and the frozen fog had an oddly luminous quality. If she hadn't been so cold and tired, Edwina would have liked to spend a minute or two just admiring it. It didn't look deadly; it was beautiful. Millions of glittering specks of ice floated in the air, sending out minute sparks of red, blue, green, and yellow, crowning and cloaking Tal in unearthly light.

She caught her breath, but the sense of wonder lasted only until she looked at his face and saw the weariness that not even his growing beard and the grime of travel could disguise. His amber eyes were sunken; his shoulders slumped. Her throat ached. Standing there, knowing her heart was in her own eyes, she looked at him and was glad that he couldn't see her. Her wind-chapped face had to be dark with campfire smoke. Her cropped hair was oily and lank. It was a small vanity, but she wanted to be attractive for him.

Swallowing back the wanting, Edwina tried her tired and aching best to be nothing more than a boy, "You want to get down now, Mr. Jones?" She cleared her throat, pitching her voice a little lower. "It looks like a good place to camp. There's a sort of a cave or a washed-out overhang."

She was talking too much and too fast. "It's big enough for us and the animals. I put the bedrolls in the back and built the fire out near the front."

"Kid," he said slowly, dismounting as he spoke, "that sounds real good."

There was something in his voice she couldn't read. It frightened her. Her heart began to hammer and her lips were so cold they didn't want to move, but she managed to squeak out, "But what? What's wrong?"

Chapter Eleven

Rock-spined and steep, the walls rose several feet overhead before being lost in the thick fog. The ravine curved to the right and deepened just beyond the narrow, rutted trail she had followed to the bottom. Partially floored with sand, the curve itself was undercut and would offer some shelter, especially if the heat from the fire reflected from the back.

There were some frozen snowdrifts against the opposite wall of the narrow canyon. She could melt the snow for water. She wasn't sure what to expect from the killer fog, but Edwina hoped the campsite would be good enough.

Judging from the way Tal was acting, whatever she found wasn't going to be enough protection. That sent new fear rushing in to gobble up what little courage she had left. She knew he hated being blind, but usually he acted like he was in full possession of his sight. Now he was behaving oddly. It was as if he knew something terrible was going to happen and that the two of them couldn't prevent it.

Taking in a shallow breath of ice-laden air, she ignored the sense of foreboding and asked again, "What is it, Mr. Jones? What's wrong?"

He cleared his throat twice. "It's cold now, and it's going to get colder. Kid, if we . . ."

She thought he swallowed hard before he went on. "If *Pogonip* takes a good hold, we might have to—to, ah, well, other folks trapped in one of these fogs have had to share a bedroll and bundle up tight to keep from freezing."

Wanting to say, but fairly sure she wouldn't be able to convince him without a valid reason, Edwina searched frantically for one he would believe. She couldn't think of anything and the silence went on too long.

"Kid, I . . ." His hand reached out toward her; she backed away. "I'm not liking it any better than you do, but, kid, we'll freeze to death if we don't."

They had been close during the ride, but sleeping in the same bed, huddled close together for warmth, was something entirely different. Anything could happen. He was sure to find out and . . . She couldn't think of a legitimate excuse to keep him out of her bed.

"No," she whispered, panic turning her denial into womanly betrayal. "No. I can't."

"Look, I know you're scared, but you have to know I wouldn't do anything to hurt you. I just . . . Dammit, kid, I . . ." He took another step toward her.

His hesitation, the expression on his face, his fumbling stutter of unfinished sentences all added up. The sum she got frightened her even more. "You think we're going to freeze to death, don't you?" she asked, not caring that the words came out harsh and full of accusation. Edwina didn't want to feel hurt or angry, but she did. The camp was far from perfect, but there was lots of wood, shelter, and water. It was the best she could do, and it really wasn't her fault they were still lost.

Tall, lean, and travel-worn, he stood there, less than three feet away, and looked at her with blind eyes. The barely healed bullet scar on his forehead was raw-looking, the skin around it gray with cold. Shivering, he pulled the quilts a little tighter around his broad shoulders and took a cautious step forward. His mouth moved, or seemed to, within the frosty tangle of his mustache and beard, but he didn't answer her accusation.

Or perhaps she just couldn't hear him. The silvery fog drank in sound and enclosed the world in muffled quiet. The silence took her breath and left her gasping. Usually so practical, her thoughts were chaotic, not settling in one place long enough to be coherent.

"Ed, I . . . Dammit all to hell, what's the matter with you?"

Edwina shivered, not sure if it was from the bitter cold or from nerves. She couldn't stop herself from saying, "Mr. Jones, I'm sorry. Truly I am."

"Sorry? For what?" Tal tried to guess where the conversation was heading but couldn't.

"It's my fault, isn't it? That we are here and . . ."

"No!"

"Yes, it is. If I could find the trail, we wouldn't be—be . . ."

It sounded like the kid was ready to cry. Tal took another step forward and reached out toward Ed. "No, it would be the same with any tenderfoot."

He licked his lips, sought for a way to tell the kid that they were going to make it back to someplace safe, but the words weren't there. They just might wander around on the desert until they starved or froze to death. "Kid," he started, "I don't know what's going to happen tomorrow, but tonight we . . ."

Ed stood between him and the fire. It leaped high, turned the fog—what little of it he could see—into a shimmer of orange-laced red. It surrounded the kid, turned him into a tall silhouette. A hat was pulled low over his ears and he was wearing a bulky coat.

While he was standing there gaping, searching for words to bolster the kid's courage and tell him they weren't dead yet, the gelding shifted its weight, put its nose between Tal's shoulder blades and shoved hard, sending him stumbling forward. Swearing, he windmilled his arms, trying to regain his balance. The quilts flapped like giant wings, spooking the horse. It crow-hopped and jumped sideways.

Stumbling forward, Tal caught the toe of his boot on rock. His arms outstretched to break his fall, his hands grabbed the front of Ed's coat, slid down, and knocked the kid backwards. By some miracle, he managed to stay on his feet.

Tal wasn't as lucky. He fell in a flutter of quilts and a storm of cuss words totally unfit for a lady's ears. He tried to get up, tangled himself in the quilts, and went down again. Somewhere in the tumult the truth went from his hands to his brain. Ed had a bosom. The kid had a . . . He wasn't a boy, he was . . . "You're a woman." Tal gasped out the words. He didn't know if he was angry or glad. "Dammit all to hell, Ed, you're a woman."

"Yes, I'm a woman." She snorted.

He thought she was crying. Wanting to comfort her and protect her from any further pain, Tal tried to get to his feet, mumbled, "Ma'am, I'm sorry. I didn't mean . . ."

He got out that much before he realized Ed was laughing. Not a simpering girlish giggle or even a ladylike titter, she was chuckling. Husky and warm, it spilled down over him.

Within seconds they were both laughing, and he, for one, didn't know why. But the shared mirth felt better than anything in a long time. When he could catch his breath, Tal got to his feet, looked at her square, and said, because it was the first thing that found its way out of his mouth, "I reckon you really are Lobo Chance. I was wrong in doubting your word like that, but, ma'am, I would like to know your real name, the one your mother calls you."

All her laughter was gone when she said, her voice flat,

without emphasis, "Edwina. Edwina Parkhurst, spinster." And then she added, in exactly the same tone, "The ground is pretty uneven. If you want I'll lead you to the bedrolls before I tend the horse."

"Miss Edwina, I . . . Why didn't you tell me? I wouldn't have . . ."

She wasn't having what he was offering. "There's nothing that needs saying now." She took his arm and practically marched him across the frozen earth. She was already turning away to take care of the evening chores when he said, "Use the horse to drag as much wood close as you can. If there's some bigger juniper logs, save them for night. It's going to get damned cold.

"Miss Parkhurst, I . . . Dammit, I . . ." His stammer just sort of hung there, waiting for him to go on, to finish whatever it was he was trying to say. He let it die. What he was feeling couldn't be said. No matter how he felt about her, he couldn't tell her. Not now. Not ever.

Sitting hunched with the quilts wrapped tight around him, Tal listened to the sounds of her labor and ached for what could never be. She was a respectable woman, and what was he? He didn't finish the thought. He didn't have to. He was fearful that he was more than half in love with her already, but even a blind gunfighter could see love wouldn't dissolve the differences that held them apart.

She grinned as she remembered the expression on Tal's face. Flabbergasted said it all. She decided she was glad he knew.

Darkness gripped them sooner than Edwina expected, bringing with it more cold. The fire wasn't putting out enough heat, not even when she was crouched over it, frying bacon and pan bread. The silence was worse than the dark.

The frozen fog had crept in closer until she could see less than a yard.

He was right about sleeping together to keep warm, but that didn't make it any easier to contemplate. Her mind repeatedly told her that wasn't a bit different than being wrapped in the same quilt and riding double on the gelding. Her body told her something else. It left her warm and wanting—and afraid.

"Ma'am." Tal's voice came out of the darkness on the other side of the fire. Startled out of her somber thoughts, Edwina jumped. The sudden movement tipped the iron frying pan to one side. Bacon grease spilled onto the glowing coals. It flamed, leaped into the pan, and set the whole thing afire. "Damn and blast," she said, dropping the whole mess to the sand as their supper turned to acrid smoke and cinders.

"Ma'am, what . . ."

Upset at herself, at him, at her burned finger, the cold, and everything else in her whole miserable world, Edwina snapped, "Stop it! Stop calling me ma'am."

She heard him get up, knew he was trying to make his way to where she stood. That made her even angrier, but only because she wanted him to. "What's wrong?" he asked. "And what in the devil is that smell?"

"Our dinner, dammit!"

"That's all?" He waited a second and then asked, "Did you . . . are you all right, ma'am? I mean, Miss Parkhurst."

"Ed," she said. "It'll be a whole lot easier if I'm still Ed, Ed Parker."

When Tal didn't answer, Edwina picked up the pan and started to scrape out the charred food. "I'll fix something else. It won't take long to cook some ham."

Hungry, weary, and cold as she was, Edwina welcomed the chance to use up more time and delay the moment when she

111

would have to go to bed. The one bed she had spread on the sheepskin-covered ground cloth. One bed for the both of them.

Colder and denser, the fog was freezing on her eyelashes by the time Edwina finished the chores and sat on the bed to remove her boots and the holstered six-gun. She was so tired and cold that she could barely move. She could probably sleep right through a ravishment. Not that she thought Tal would do such a thing. No, he might be a gunfighter and a man who would send her mother into a swoon at the very sight of him, but he was a man of honor. She knew that with her heart and her mind.

She was the one she couldn't trust, Edwina thought, a bit wryly. She tucked the boots under the edge of the pallet to keep them from freezing and, taking the revolver with her, she crawled fully clothed in beside the silent man.

Tal reached up, pulled part of the ground cloth over their heads to shelter them from the ravages of *Pogonip*. Holding herself stiffly, careful not to touch him, she lay there, her back toward him, without moving until the warmth generated by his body seeped into her. It gradually relaxed her tense muscles and sent her into a half doze. Full sleep was less than a breath away when he turned toward her, rose to one elbow, and slid his other hand across her face, clamping it on her mouth.

Before she could do much more than make a muffled protest, Tal whispered, "Shhhhhh. Listen. Something's coming down the trail."

Heart pounding, straining to hear, she nodded in understanding. He removed his hand from her mouth, setting her free to fumble for the six-shooter with a shaking hand. She wanted to beat a fast retreat from the new danger that threatened.

Outlaws? Indians? Bears? *Lejubes?* Her mind jumping from one conjecture to the next, Edwina raised the ground cloth and peeked out. She could see nothing but the fog. Thick, cold, and smothering, it had absorbed the orange of the fire and turned it sullen and threatening.

She couldn't see what was creeping up on them, but she could hear it. More than one of something bigger than a coyote, heavier than the antelope. But what? Almost too frightened to breathe, Edwina lifted the cloth a little higher, cocked the six-gun, and waited. She listened as the creatures crunched across the frozen sand toward where the gelding and the mule were tied.

The sounds stopped. Nothing happened for several seconds. Pent breath burning in her chest, Edwina fought against dizziness, tried to force her fear-paralyzed lungs to expel the air, and gulp in more. They did, just enough so that she could choke back a scream of terror when demonic sounds clawed their way through the canyon. The sound bounced and echoed for what seemed an eternity before the heart-stopping chorus began again.

EEEEEeeeeeeee-yyyaaaaaaaaaahhhhhhh! Eeeeeeeeeeeee-yaaaaaaaaaah!

The demons yowled like Satan's fiends. The noise rammed into the walls and was flung back, seeming come from everywhere and nowhere.

Edwina got to her knees. Shaking with fear and cold, trying desperately to aim in the direction of the danger, she pointed the wavering revolver. She strained to distinguish shapes in the fog.

Tal was yelling something, but she couldn't understand what he was saying. His words were lost in the terrible on-slaught of unearthly sound.

"What is it?" she shouted, but her desperate question was

lost in the cries of the braying demons. Ready to defend them both, her forefinger tightened on the trigger.

Shouting "Don't shoot!" Tal struggled free of the quilts, grabbed her from behind, and tilted the gun barrel toward the sky.

Scared witless by the hellish noise, she fought with him for control of the revolver. His mouth only inches from her ear, Tal yelled a single word. It took an eon for the sense of it to penetrate her fear. "Burros?" she asked blankly. "What are . . . oh, I . . . oh."

Still shaking, her heart beating wildly, Edwina lowered the weapon. She let it dangle between lax fingers and waited for her body to believe what her mind had learned. Not Tal's demons. Not even his *tum tum wawas*. Nothing to be afraid of. Burros.

Not knowing whether to laugh or cry, teeth chattering too hard to do either, she eased the hammer down, fumbled with icy fingers until the six-gun was safely back in the holster. She didn't fight when Tal pressed on her shoulders, silently urging her to return to the warmth of the bed.

They were under the quilts, the ground cloth giving them some protection from the freezing fog, when the manic braying stopped and the echoes softened and died. Still shivering, sure she would never be warm again, Edwina managed to voice the worry that had risen to plague her, "The burros, are they . . . Is someone with them? I mean, was there? A traveler? Lost or . . ."

"No. They're wild. I don't know how they got here originally. Likely they came down into the canyon for shelter." And then he said, "Ed, I'm not trying to pull anything, but you've got to get warm and the only way to do that is . . ." He put his arm around her, gathering her close.

"No, I . . . Mr. Jones, you . . ."

He ignored her protests, held her closer, and said, his voice deep and impersonal, "Ed, about that little book we were writing. The one you called *Lurkers in the Canyon*. Do you suppose we should be doing a little more thinking about it and the one that comes after? Likely you're going to need both of them to finish that contract when we get back to Winnemucca. It'll be easier writing if we scrape off the rough spots."

The cold was relentless. It crept under the edges of their covering and chilled all it touched, but Edwina's shivering finally stopped and she was able to respond to his questions. Just how sensible her responses were, she wasn't at all sure, but she knew that she trusted him. The trust and her own terrible weariness lulled her, slurred her words, and sent her headlong into dreamless sleep.

"How long do these fogs last? The wood is almost gone and our animals are getting restless. I moved the picket line again, but those miserable burros—and there's a whole herd of them—have just about demolished the rabbit brush. The terrible little beasts even tried to tear open the packs," she said, coming back from her morning round of chores.

His sight had improved slightly and now Tal had chores of his own—tasks he had demanded and, he thought with a grin, jobs she hadn't been loath to give him. Taking sagebrush from the pile beside him, Tal added it to the fire before he answered. "This is what? The second day? Well, it should be lifting soon. Maybe this afternoon or tomorrow."

He heard her get out the frying pan and start muttering mild curses under her breath as she hacked off pieces of frozen ham to cook for their breakfast. Smiling at her choice of words, he cleared his throat and mentioned what he had been pondering.

"Ed, in the night I thought I heard voices. Three, maybe more, men on horseback. Maybe it was a dream, but I swear I heard them complaining about the fog. I heard the horses too, but . . ."

Quitting what she was doing, Ed came over to stand before him. "Why didn't you wake me?"

"I was going to, but strange things go on out here on the desert. It could have been a trick of sound. Kid, I can't swear I wasn't dreaming, but I just wanted to tell you so you would be on guard."

"Outlaws?"

"I don't know. Whoever is out there, I pity the poor devils. *Pogonip* is no respecter of man or beast, but if they're out there, we can't fire a gun or anything to lead them here."

He could almost feel her bristle, and her voice had real bite when she snarled, "Because I'm not a boy?"

"No," he said, glancing up at her and wishing he could see her face, "because of what happened to your sister. Ed, I was going to take a man's money to see that those wagons and what was in them got through safe. I didn't do that, but I will do whatever is necessary to get you back to civilization.

"Bringing strangers into our camp isn't the right way to go about that. If they were really out there, we don't know who they are and—"

Her voice hadn't gotten any gentler when she asked, "If it was just you, what would you do? What if they aren't outlaws but are just travelers? Mr. Jones, tell me the truth, would you leave them out in this—" he thought she made a sweeping gesture that encompassed the fog—"to freeze or wander around lost."

It wasn't something he needed to think about, but he hesitated before he answered. "No, Ed, if things were like they were before, I reckon I'd do my best to—"

"That's what I thought." Whirling around, she stomped off.

He heard the snick of a hammer being thumbed back, and leaped up. "What in the hell are you doing? You can't call them in here."

"Why not?" she asked, her voice sounding too sweet by half. "Because I'm a slab-sided, vinegar-tongued old maid who has to be delivered to her brother-in-law in order for you to get paid?"

"Slab-sided?" Disbelief was strong in his voice. "Ed, by my reckoning, and I ought to know, you are—"

"What?" The anger had gone out of her voice, leaving an odd undertone.

"Beautiful," he said softly, knowing the truth in the word even before it left his mouth. "Miss Edwina Parkhurst, you are beautiful."

Her laugh was young and innocent. There was nothing but warmth in her voice when she reminded him, "You, Mr. Talmadge Jones, are blind."

He wanted to say, "Only my eyes," but he didn't. "My being blind is the reason I didn't want to announce our presence. Not because you're a woman. There's no way I could protect you if they were outlaws."

"I see," Edwina said, understanding him more clearly.

Chapter Twelve

A burro snorted and another squealed. The fire snapped. Embers cracked explosively and sent out a shower of firefly sparks. The horse whuffled softly and stamped his feet. Other than the sound of ham sizzling in the pan and his own breathing, Tal could hear nothing of any import.

If there had been riders out on the desert during the night, they were gone now—and he couldn't help feeling relief. Men traveling at night with *Pogonip* prowling the land were either riding on the wrong side of the law or damn fools. Both choices turned his thoughts sour. Neither outlaws nor fools would do Edwina any good—and were far more likely to do her harm.

Either the fog was thinning a little or else his sight was improving because, even at several feet away, he could see her. Not distinctly, but enough to distinguish a fire-touched blur where her face would be. Despite the harsh restraints he had placed on it, his wanting escaped. He hungered to trace the angle of her jaw and the set of her eyes with his fingertips and his lips.

Almost painfully aware of her every movement and of his need to protect her at all costs—even from himself—Tal heard her slide the revolver into the holster she wore strapped around her waist before she turned the ham in the frying pan.

"You know," she said, sounding surprised and a little put

out, "I used to really like ham."

"Me, too," he said, glad of anything that would lighten the fear that lurked at the back of his mind. They were lost and would either starve to death or freeze before he could get her somewhere safe and find help for her missing sister. "And pan bread, even if it had some ash to give it flavor, wasn't the worse thing I ever tasted either, especially if you had some sorghum to slather on it."

"That's true." She sighed. "What would you have if we . . . if you were someplace warm and could have anything in the world to eat?"

He didn't have to think about it. Her idle question had already conjured an image and it was enough to make him drool like a teething babe. "A steak, big enough to cover a plate, and soda biscuits dripping with real butter and maybe some peach preserves like my mother used to make. Yeah, and some spuds fried with onions." He swallowed and added, "And pie."

"Oh, yes! Pie," she said. "Hot apple pie with thick cream poured over it and—" She stopped, stood, and turned to look toward the canyon rim. "What was that?"

"I didn't—"

"Shhhh. Listen."

He heard it. Faint, but it had to be a shot. After a heartbeat, another sounded. Somebody was out there. He hoped to hell it wasn't the outlaws, but if it was, there was no turning back now. Likely, outlaws wouldn't be firing signaling shots anyway.

The frying pan made a grating sound as she pulled it from its bed of coals. She asked, "Had I better shoot so they'll know . . . ?"

"Wait."

"But—"

Looking toward her, he chose his words with care, wanting to keep her on her toes, but not wanting to frighten her. "Kid, I don't know who's out there. It could be good folk, and probably it is, but I think you'd better keep on . . . I believed you were a boy, but . . ."

"Ed, what do you really look like? Will they know you're not what you're claiming to be?"

"Mr. Jones, you don't need to worry on my account. My face is so grimy with smoke and dirt that even my own mother wouldn't know me. If I have to, I imagine I can fool whoever it is until we get to a place where it no longer matters."

After a moment, she added, "It's you that's the problem. You've been acting differently toward me since you found out. Mr. Jones, we have to go on if we can and find help. Olivia is a sanctimonious fool, but she's my sister. Maybe it's too late to do anything, but I have to at least try."

"Yeah. I know. Dammit, kid, I just wanted to . . ." He stopped, took a deep breath, and said, "Maybe you'd better go ahead and shoot."

They listened intently after Edwina fired three shots, but there was no answer.

Still not warm, but not as cold as he had been, Tal waited until they ate breakfast and she had cleared the remains before he voiced his thought. "Seems like I can hear the wind whimpering and crying again. Is the fog lifting?"

"It's still thick down here, but I'll climb out of the canyon and look."

"Be careful going up and don't—"

She chuckled before she said, "I'm a boy, remember. Boys aren't supposed to have enough sense to be careful and nobody actually expects them to, do they?"

He threw some wood on the fire and stood up. "Yeah, well, I'm a blind gunslinger, remember, mean as hell, a purely selfish bastard and a cold-blooded killer not giving a damn for anybody or anything but myself. Being that, I wouldn't want anything to happen to a fuzz-faced kid who is all the eyes I have, would I?"

Her voice rode a little higher, shook a little before it steadied. "Mr. Jones, you're not mean and—"

"No? Ask anyone who ever tried to cross me. I haven't been in this part of Nevada for long, but word gets around about men like me. Folks walk and talk carefully around me, in order not to rile me. Don't ever forget it, kid.

"I am . . . was a gunfighter. I've killed men. Maybe some of them got what was coming to them, but a gunfighter doesn't have friends."

"Oh," she said, then muttered something before she spun around and stalked away.

Edwina knew he was telling the truth. She also suspected it hadn't been easy for him to say it. She knew things he hadn't mentioned, like his honor, his courage, and his ability to make the worst of situations bearable. It didn't matter that he was a gunfighter; if he had been in one of the old tales, Tal would have been the hero with the gentle heart.

Drawing in a shuddery breath, fighting against the ache in her throat, and blinking back the tears that burned her eyes, Edwina clenched her hands into fists. Stopping at the base of the trail, she turned to look back through the fog.

It was thinning, not a lot but enough so that she could see his dark shape standing between her and the fire. *Pogonip* was still an adversary to be reckoned with, but its ice crystals had dwindled in size and were moving slightly with each nudge of a small breeze.

Hopeful the worst was over, she ascended the steep slope. Not wanting to tumble headlong back into the ravine and leave Tal alone to face the desert, she set her feet carefully and climbed slowly. Gaining the rim, Edwina wasn't sure things were better.

It was still foggy. The crystals had frozen on everything, turning every rock, bush, leaf, and twig ice white. Then it froze even more crystals on top of the ice, building up and up until the whole world was a fuzzy white. White on white, crystalline lace endlessly repeating, there was so much sameness she couldn't gauge distances. She was disappointed until she glanced up and saw a pale circle of gold.

The circle grew bolder as she watched, turning the white world shades of rose-gold. The wind took heart, puffed and blew. Between them, they harried *Pogonip* until Edwina knew it was going to disappear before the day was much older.

Eddying and swirling, the fog curled and writhed, opening narrow alleys or broad roads, giving brief glimpses of the surrounding country, and just as quickly hiding them away. Edwina saw a trail of hoofprints made by shod hooves and not burros. A trail their own beasts had not made on their way into the ravine.

"Ed! Ed? Dammit, boy, where are you?"

Tal's call was faint, but it was enough to send Edwina hurrying back to tell him of her discovery. After a rapid consultation they packed what remained of their dwindling supplies onto the feisty mule, saddled the gelding, and bid farewell to the canyon that had sheltered them from the killer fog.

The fog had lifted earlier, leaving behind clear skies and above freezing temperatures. Taking advantage of the change, they had ridden as far as possible, following the trail left by the horsemen.

It was nearing dark when Edwina saw the pinpoint of orange in the distance. "Mr. Jones," she said quietly, reining in the plodding gelding and taking a deep breath to still the excitement that was growing with every beat of her heart. "It looks like we found the travelers."

"Walk in slow," he said, sitting up a little straighter behind her and letting the quilt that had covered them both fall away from her. "Have your six-gun where you can reach it, but don't draw unless you have to. Kid, remember what I told you: If you have to shoot, shoot to kill. You don't usually have a second chance."

Swallowing the lump in her throat, Edwina meant every word. "Yes, sir, I will." But she waited a second longer before she flicked the gelding with the reins and set him into motion again.

"Keep your eyes open and tell me what you see."

Tersely given, it was an order she obeyed, even though her mouth got drier and the empty feeling in her middle increased with every step. "They have got a big fire going and something is cooking. There are shadows moving around the fire. Men, I guess, lots of them."

"How many?" he asked with his lips close to her ear.

Edwina started to answer, saw something else, and the count lodged in her mouth, dissolved, and was replaced by a startled exclamation. "No! It can't be!"

"What?" And when she didn't answer immediately, he asked again, "What? Dammit, Ed, what's the matter now?" He put his hands on her shoulders and gave them a gentle shake.

"Oh, Mr. Jones, I think it's our camp."

"What do you mean, our camp? We're not back in the big canyon, are we?"

"Not there, I mean, our camp. Olivia's and mine. The one where the outlaws attacked and—and you were shot."

"How do you know?"

She told him what she could see, the stark shadows black

against the leaping flames. "The freight wagons. The one the outlaws burned and the one that didn't have any whiskey in it. They're both still there. Maybe we'd better not go . . ."

Her words came too late. They had been sighted by the men in the camp, and three of them had mounted up and were riding out to meet them.

Swallowing hard, sure they were destined for the same doom that had struck down the muleskinners, she whispered, "They're coming for us. They're armed. Oh, Mr. Jones, what shall I do?"

"Long about now," he said, giving her shoulders a little reassuring squeeze, "there's not a lot you can do except keep riding toward them. Don't let 'em spook you into turning tail and running—that's a good way to get us shot. Understand?"

Nodding, she took a deep breath and tried to still the shivers that were starting in her stomach. "Yes, sir," she said, wincing a little as it came out as a squeak.

"Ed," he said, his voice low, "I reckon I'm about as scared as you are, but we can't let them know it." Tal paused a moment before adding, "Kid, keep your mouth shut and let me do the talking."

She had to be content with that. She halted the gelding when the men drew up in front of them and the one in the middle, a large, bearded man in a soiled blanket coat, asked, in a deep, mellow voice, "You the fellas that was doing the shooting earlier?"

Afraid her tongue would betray her, Edwina nodded.

"A couple of us rode out and did a mite of looking, but there weren't no telling which way to be going."

She nodded again.

"Lost, are you?" the same man asked.

"Lost and blind," Tal said, his voice almost hard, clearly demanding no pity. He shifted so he could be seen around her shoulder and asked a question of his own, sounding colder and meaner than she would have believed possible, "The kid's a tenderfoot. I got shot in the head. If the kid's got sense enough to be telling me the truth, it happened here. You're not the no-count bastards that did the shooting, are you?"

"So, that's what happened, was it? Indians?"

"No."

"This here ain't where Raiter's missing booze was hijacked, is it?" asked a second man, sounding eager. He was smaller than the first, but equally soiled and bearded.

Twilight deepened and was close to turning full dark; a dark half moon was rising to combat. The wind died to an icy whisper that only added to the pulse of fear that beat in Edwina's veins. She was warned back into silence by Tal's fingers squeezing her arm.

Evidently the warning was for her alone, because Jones said, his voice giving nothing away, "Yes, I reckon this must be the place."

The man kneed his mare, brought her forward three or four paces, eyed Tal narrowly, and said, satisfaction fairly oozing from his words, "By crackies, I knew it. I seen you once down in Santa Fe. You be that missing gunslinger Raiter hired, ain't you? Jones? The one he's talking about, blaming for everythin' that's happened around these parts since Eve gave Adam that damned apple?"

"I'm Jones," Tal said.

"Lordy, man, what happened? Your outlaw pards shoot you and leave you for dead like them other poor devils we found back at camp?"

"Too bad it wasn't Raiter himself out here," the third man said flatly. He was slightly behind the first man, so Edwina couldn't see him clearly, but she thought he was taller than the other two and leaner. Whatever he looked like, there was no mistaking the anger in his voice. It was directed at her brother-in-law.

The first man took charge. "You do any of the shooting here?"

"Nope," Tal answered.

"How about you, kid? That six-gun of yours looks like it's there for business you do any of the shooting here?"

Edwina started to answer, again Tal stopped her. "No," he said. "Ed didn't do any shooting."

"I asked him," the man said, not mean, but as if he fully intended to get an answer. He looked at Edwina and said, "Well."

She wasn't sure what to do, so she sat there, stared back at him for a long moment without saying anything. The wind picked up again. The gelding took a step forward.

The man's rifle lifted. It was pointed straight at her chest. His forefinger curled around the trigger and it tightened as she watched. Terrified, certain he was going to shoot her dead within the next few seconds, Edwina whispered, trying her best to sound like a boy, but too frightened to be convincing, "Mister, Olivia Raiter is my sister. I wouldn't shoot . . . They took her . . ."

"What the hell are you talking about? They took Who?"

"My sister. Her two girls. They took them with the wagons. I—I don't know if they're hurt or . . . I was . . ." She couldn't tell the truth, not all of it, but she had to say something.

Taking a deep breath, Edwina plunged on, hoping the man wasn't going to shoot them before she could get out some sort of explanation. "Olivia was mad at me. We had an argument and—and I—I ran off. I was in the canyon when the outlaws . . ." Her voice broke.

"Raiter didn't say nothing about a wife or a little brother

being with them wagons," the second man said. "All he said was some calico queens was coming for the upstairs and bringing more whiskey. You sure you ain't lying, sonny?"

"He knew Olivia and the girls were coming. He sent for them, but he didn't know I was coming," Edwina said. "I didn't want to come. Ambrose doesn't like me. But Mama sent me along so Olivia and the girls wouldn't have to travel out here alone."

The man started to ask something else, but Tal cut him off. "You planning on making us stay out here all night in the cold, answering fool questions that could just as easily be answered by the fire?"

The rifle stayed steady, the business end still pointing at Edwina's chest, until the man said, "I don't know Raiter, but I've heard tales. Milch here"—he jerked his head toward the smaller man—"claims to know him personal but that don't make no never-mind now. Come on in and get some grub in your bellies."

"Thanks," Tal said. Edwina breathed easier when the rifle barrel was turned so the weapon rested across the man's forearm. She gave the reins a little slap against the gelding's neck, urging him forward.

Wheeling their mounts, the strangers fell in beside them, two on one side, one—the large man in the blanket coat—on the other. He said, "Name's Jake Larson. Case is my brother. The other fella is Orson Milch—he joined up with us at Raiter's place. We was just passing through, coming from the mines in Idaho, going to California, when we heard the news and decided to do a little prospecting for the reward." That said, he waited for them to introduce themselves.

Tal obliged him. "Tal Jones," he said, and then added, sounding like it was only an afterthought, "The kid's Ed. Ed Parker."

They rode into camp, passing between the burned wagon and the one that still held a few fluttering rags of dirty canvas and trunks filled with Olivia's treasured goods.

Edwina was glad when Tal climbed off the gelding and ordered her, like she was a stable boy, to take care of the animals and spread their bedrolls before she came to supper. Edwina said, trying to sound like a sullen boy, "Yes, sir," before she looked over at Jake and said, "Jones can't see worth a damn. Better watch to see he doesn't walk straight into the fire."

She climbed stiffly off the horse and led him and the mule over to the picket line, walking beside Case who looked like he intended to care for the rest of the beasts. He stomped along beside her, but he wasn't acting like he meant to do any talking. He worked silently until the animals had been fed, and she had covered the mule and gelding for the night. When she leaned over to pick up the pack, Case Larson grabbed her by the arm, jerked her close, and said, his voice too low to carry more than a foot or two, "You're jumpy as hell, kid. What are you up to? What're you and that damned gunslinger trying to hide?"

"Nu-nu-nothing," she managed to stammer as he leaned closer, stared at her, and then twisted his lips into a cold, knowing smile. It said, "You aren't fooling me. I know exactly who and what both of you are."

Fear cramping in her stomach, Edwina was shaking so hard she could hardly stand when he released her, turned, and stalked off into the moon-bright night.

"Please," she whispered, her mouth too dry for the small plea to escape. "Please, don't." Staring after him as he disappeared from sight, she wasn't sure just what it was he thought he knew. She did know she was terribly afraid.

Chapter Thirteen

"Hey, kid!"

The gravelly voice caught her attention. Taking a deep breath, steeling herself to face some new trouble, Edwina turned and looked toward the men gathered around the fire. The shift of shadow and light made them difficult to count but she thought there were ten or eleven, not including Tal. He was sitting on a rock, holding a tin cup that sent up a small cloud of steam.

"Dammit, kid, quit'cha mooning around. Drop your gear someplace and get over here if you want some of this here grub a-fore I throw it out. You hear what I'm a-saying, kid?"

"Yes, sir, I . . . Yes, sir." With a quick glance in the direction Case Larson had taken, Edwina compelled her unwilling body to move. Larson couldn't know anything about her, she told herself. He was just trying to scare her. He had to be.

The wind tugged at her hat, her coat, and nipped her ears. Shivering, Edwina sighed. The men were talking, laughing, and swearing.

Ignoring the profanity, she picked up the bedrolls and what was left of the supplies and stumbled across the uneven ground to an empty space near the blazing campfire. Once there, she remembered enough boyish behavior to act in character. Dropping their belongings in a careless heap, Ed Parker hurried to get some food.

It was a meal she wasn't sure she could eat. She was hungry, or she had been before Case had grabbed her arm. Now Edwina wasn't sure the fear that had her by the throat would allow her swallow.

She straightened her back and even managed a quick, "Thanks," to the short, grizzled man who handed her a loaded plate.

Sharing Tal's rock, she took a small spoonful of the offering. It melted in her mouth and went down easy, leaving her surprised at the size of her growing appetite. The corn pone, fried in bacon grease and far too salty, and the venison stew, scraped out of the bottom of the communal pot and rich with onions, were the best food Edwina had tasted in ages. She was tempted to hold the battered tin plate up to her mouth and shovel the food in with her hands.

Hunched over, her hat hiding most of her face, she was chewing away, enjoying every bite, until one of the miners said, "Jones, you really a gunfighter like Milch said?"

"I was." Tal's voice was cold, hard, and rather threatening. Edwina stopped chewing. Alert, her heart beginning to speed up, she was intensely aware of the man beside her. She knew how dangerous he could be, but she didn't raise her head or even glance at him.

"You ever meet that Lobo Chance? That fancy gunslinger what writes them little books?"

"No. Why?" A little of the chill was gone, leaving a trace of curiosity in Tal's question.

"We been wandering all over hell's half-acre for the last week or more, a-looking for his dang-blasted sorry hide. We ain't seen us nary a whisker, and I was just a-wondering if you'd a-seen him. I reckon the finding of him would be a heap easier iffen we knew what he looked like. You know, iffen he really wears them fancy duds, them white buckskin shirts and leather britches he talks about in them books. And them silver six-guns. I'd be real partial to seeing something like that."

What she was hearing didn't make any sense. "Why are you looking for Lobo Chance?" The words were out of her mouth before she could snatch them back, but Edwina, flustered and wary, managed to duck her head before the speaker looked in her direction.

"You be knowing him then, kid?"

"I—I . . ." There was no reason for anyone, except her publisher, to know Lobo Chance had gone west. Why would these men be looking for him?

If her mother found out the truth from the newspapers or the publisher before they found Olivia, it would be . . . Sickness clutched her stomach and squeezed it tight. She searched frantically for something to say. "My mother doesn't allow dime novels in the house. She says they are the devil's work and the preacher . . ."

"Then why was Chance traveling with you and your sister instead of taking the stage out of Winnemucca like ordinary folks? If he was traveling with you, you have to know something about him, don't you?"

She knew that voice. Case Larson had returned to the fire and was staring at her, waiting for her answer. Lifting her chin, she returned his stare and said, flatly, "He wasn't with us."

Slow and deadly, Case walked toward her. His voice gave her the shivers. "Damn lying kid, I oughta slap some—"

The words were barely out of Case's mouth before Tal was on his feet, his right hand loose and ready, hovering over his six-gun. "I wouldn't try it, Larson, unless you fancy a bellyful of lead."

Case's answer was a mean-sounding laugh. He said, "You

ain't a gunfighter no more, Jones. You're a blind good-for-nothing, and I'm gonna—"

Jake Larson intervened. He hurried around the campfire. "Hell, Jones, there's no sense getting riled about this. Well, the truth of it is Case talks too damned much, and thinks too damned little. Why don't you finish your grub and forget it. Case didn't mean any real harm to the kid."

Tal wasn't that easily mollified. "What the hell is going on around here?" he asked. "What's all this fuss about Lobo Chance? The man can't write worth beans and besides that he's a pie-headed idiot, who—"

"Who's worth a cool thousand dollars to whoever finds him," Jake said. His voice rose above the babble of the miners as each gave his own version of why they were out on the high desert in the middle of winter looking for a famous gunfighter by the name of Lobo Chance.

Edwina was astonished. A thousand dollars? It couldn't be true. Nothing made any sense to her. One of the miners had found some pages in the ravine and concluded that Lobo Chance had been with them. Her publisher was taking a chance on exposing her for the publicity. It had to be for publicity because there wasn't anyone who actually cared what happened to Lobo Chance. On the other hand, she cared about what might be going to happen to Tal if Jake couldn't get his brother to back down

Tal was still tense and ready to draw. Case Larson didn't look like he was changing his mind either. Shaking but knowing what she had to do, Edwina took a deep breath. She set her plate on a rock, stood up slowly, and took her place at Tal's side. Imitating his stance, she was ready to draw and shoot whenever he did.

Her hands were icy. Her stomach was threatening to reject the food she had just eaten. Her heart was beating so fast and hard it hurt, but despite the shaking that was rocking her knees like baby cradles, Edwina was ready. Her voice was steady when she said, "As you said, Mr. Jones is at a disadvantage at the moment. I'm not blind, Mr. Larson, and I wouldn't take kindly to you shooting Mr. Jones."

Time slowed down and everything got clear. She could see the way the shadows danced in and out of the leaping flames and the fire color on Case's beard, turning it dark red with glints of gold. The wind seemed to be taking short breaths and huffing a bit.

"Case!" Jake's voice rose. He walked over in front of his brother. "Dammit, Case, back off. The kid didn't—"

"The lying little bastard needs a lesson in manners, and I intend to see that he—"

Tal wasn't ready to call it quits either. "Touch the kid and you're dead, Larson. Ed's not a liar and he's not a bastard, so I reckon you got some apologizing to do."

"He's hiding something. I—"

"Case," his brother said warningly, "that's enough. The kid hasn't done anything to make you—"

Milch broke into the conversation. "We come out here looking for Chance, knowing we was chasing after a mighty wild goose, but a-hoping to strike it richer than we did back at the mines. Now, boys, I've been thinking, and, by howdies, I'm guessing Raiter might be real thankful to see them whiskey wagons of his. Real thankful."

There was a chorus of agreement. The chorus grew louder when Jake Larson said, "I reckon none of us would turn down a reward like that publisher back east is planning on giving whoever finds Chance, but this thing with the wagons troubles me."

He clapped his brother on the shoulder. "What say, Case, want to rescue some whiskey and some ladies?"

133

Case glared at him for a long moment and then nodded. "Yeah. Maybe it won't be for nothing. Likely that Chance was took with the women. Maybe we get them all at once."

Dizzy with relief and sure she was going to swoon, Edwina swayed. Tal hissed, "Breathe, dammit. It's over." But she felt new sickness wash over her when he added, speaking for her alone, "For now."

The worry was buried under a heavy cloak of weariness by the time she cleaned up after the meal, rustled up some more wood for the night fire, and spread Tal's bedroll and her own several feet away. When she was finished, Edwina returned to her place at Tal's side to listen to what was being said by the miners. Hardcases, but there was a curious respect when they talked about Olivia and the girls.

"Don't you worry none, kid," the cook told Edwina, "we'll save that sister of yourn and them girls of hern, too. Hell, we'll shoot the lights and livers out of them outlaws." He chortled at the very thought before he added, "And I reckon Raiter won't miss a keg or two of that rotgut them fellers stole. I could use me a big long drink of that. Yes, sireee, I could."

Someone else, sitting on the other side of the fire, laughed and said, "Hell, we might even give you a shot or two, iffen you put that gun of yourn to some good use. Hell, kid, you never know, some drinking likker might help put some meat on your bones."

"Jones and the kid won't be there to do any shooting, or any drinking either," Jake Larson said, speaking from the far side of the fire.

"Why the hell not?" the cook asked, looking toward him and sounding a little irritated. "Miz Raiter's the kid's sister, and he's toting iron like he knows how to use it."

"It doesn't make any difference what he wants," Larson

said. "Jones is blind. He can't do anything but get in the way of the rest of us. I'm gonna leave him at the first ranch we pass. Him and the kid both."

"I reckon we'd be better off to take them with us. They're both hiding something and—"

"Case," his brother said, "I keep hoping you'll get some sense, but likely it ain't going to happen any time soon."

Another man added, "Iffen we're gonna get up early, I reckon as how we oughta be turning in." He stood up, stretched, and ambled away from the fire.

Within minutes, everyone except the man standing first watch had followed his advice. Knowing full well he didn't actually need her help, but feeling better just being close to him, Edwina guided Tal to his bedroll, and nodded when he whispered, "Be careful, kid, and watch your back."

"You, too," she said as she walked to her own bedding.

His sight was improving more than he was letting on, but that small blessing didn't keep the next couple of days from being hell.

Tal swore that he spent part of every minute setting his jaw, swallowing hot words, and keeping sane enough not to draw on the whole damn pack of miners and shooting them. They believed Edwina was a boy and thought she ought to be working off her keep as well as Tal's. She was assigned every dirty job in camp.

She did it without complaining. Tal knew her shoulders had to be aching and her hands hurting, and he couldn't even rub the pain out of those muscles. He couldn't even talk to her without Case Larson listening, as though he suspected they were planning a robbery or a murder.

There wasn't much to see even if his sight was improving. He knew they were following the tracks left by Raiter's stolen wagons and traveling quickly, except through the stretches where the storms had erased the trail and they had to search for it.

Tal's horse was tied to the back of the cart Ed was driving, and Tal went where it led. By the afternoon of the second day Tal was drooping in the saddle. For Edwina's sake he hoped the miners found a ranch before they found the outlaws, but ranches were few on the high desert. Outlaws were easier to come by. And the ones they were following weren't going to give up without a fight.

Slumping a little more, Tal sighed. The whole country was hills, plateaus, canyons, playa, and more hills. Dark as his thoughts, the sky was hanging low. It looked like it might be breeding another storm and Tal was already cold.

Warned by the hoofbeats of a galloping horse, he jerked his head up and listened intently. He knew Jake Larson feared an ambush and had sent riders to scout ahead. A hoarse shout announced the outlaws had turned the wagons and headed into a wide-mouthed box canyon not more than a mile ahead.

His horse stopped when Ed reined in the mules. Tal dismounted and stood at the back of the wagon, listening to the excited miners making plans. They were all ready to go rushing into the canyon with guns blazing.

"We'll get Miz Raiter and them gals o' hern outta there before sunset," one of them yelled.

"Yeah, and grab old Lobo Chance while we're at it," another shouted.

"Come on, boys, let's go!"

"Dammit, stay where you are. We're not going nowhere until we find out if they are really in that canyon or not," Jake said, not yelling, but raising his voice and turning the din to silence.

One of the men said, "Dammit, use your eyes. There ain't

but one set o' tracks going in and none coming out."

The arguments started. Taking a chance they were too occupied to notice, Tal walked to the front of the cart. "Kid," he said, talking low and not looking in her direction, "there's about to be a lot of dying when they go in after those outlaws. Whatever you do, don't let those idiots talk you into—"

"Talk him into what, Jones?" Case asked, coming up behind Tal.

Tal turned and stared at the man.

"Well, Jones, you afraid the kid will tell us the truth now to save his own miserable hide?"

The miners had turned to hear Case. "What truth is that, Case?" Tal asked. "That I don't want the kid riding into trouble with a pack of fools?"

Case snorted. "Naw, Jones, I reckon you're afraid the kid will tell us that you were with the outlaws all the time. You afraid of that, Jones?"

Case's brother, Jake, snarled, "That's enough, Case."

Someone else interrupted. "Be that right, kid? Was Jones with that bunch of owlhoots?"

Edwina jumped down off the cart and faced the mob. "Those men took my sister and her girls. If you think I would travel with one of them, then maybe we need to get something settled right now. I said Mr. Jones wasn't with them. If anyone wants to question my honesty, I would be happy to oblige them with . . ."

What if Case or one of the others decided to use their fists? He eased over to stand beside her, knowing that he could probably shoot one or two of them . . .

"Damnation, kid, we didn't mean no insult. I reckon Hiram here spoke outta turn," one of the men said.

"That's right," Jake seconded. "We need to be figgering on how we're going to smoke out the outlaws. Right, Case?"

"Yeah, I reckon, but I'm telling you for fair, kid, that when this is over, you and I are going to have this out."

"Fine," Edwina said.

"Ed," Tal warned.

"Kid," Case drawled, obviously not meaning a word of it, "I reckon I was wrong about Jones being one of the outlaws."

"You were," she said, a satisfied note in her voice.

"I reckon, too," Case said smoothly, "since Miz Raiter is your sister, you'll be right up front, with that six-gun of yourn blazing, when we go in."

Jake Larson tried to say something, so did Tal, but neither one of them were quick enough to stop Edwina from agreeing. "Where else would I be?"

"That's the ticket, kid," one of the men said with a loud laugh.

"You bet," another added.

"Now that that's settled," Jake said, "we ought to do a little planning."

Agreeing with Jake's words, the miners walked back to their horses, listening to Jake give orders as they went.

Tal only had time to hiss, "You be careful, Ed, and don't do something foolish." He knew he sounded mean, but that's the way he felt. She had been tricked into something that might get her killed, and there wasn't a damned thing he could do to change it.

Chapter Fourteen

Oooooowwwwhhhhhhhhhhhhh.

The plaintive howl crawled through the canyons and echoed from the hills. The wild cry was an omen of impending doom, and Edwina knew it in the part of her that rejected rational thought.

Drawing on all the old tales she had ever heard, she knew what it meant. Someone she loved was going to die.

The two red mules acted like they knew it, too.

The big one stopped in his tracks and jerked the other to a halt before he threw up his head, laid back his ears, and bared ugly yellow teeth. Standing too close to the eye-rolling beast for her own peace of mind, Edwina wanted to release the harness strap and run.

She wanted to run as fast and as far as she could. Run until she hadn't enough breath or strength left to take another step, and then cry like the bereft animal was crying.

"Them critters ain't close enough to do us any hurt. Don't let 'em spook you, kid," the cook growled, sounding like the howl had also upset him a little. "We gotta git hid out in that little ravine before it gets full dark."

"Yes, sir," Edwina whispered. She looked back. Tal sat on the gelding, a tempting target. He should have been walking beside the cart, using it to guide him, but Jake had decreed otherwise.

She was expected to do as she was told and to keep her mouth shut.

The sooner they got into the ravine, the sooner Tal could have a little more protection. Edwina took a deep breath, tugged on the strap, and tried to convince the balky mule to move. He set his feet and refused. "Come on," she said and jerked at the harness again.

"You need to talk to him in words he understands." Leading his own horse, the short, skinny cook—everybody called him Crock, but she thought his name was Crocker—came up behind her. He gave the recalcitrant mule a re-sounding whack on the shoulder and some rather fierce and colorful instructions to get moving or have a fire built under his rump. It did the trick too well.

The mule plunged forward, dragging Edwina. Her feet skittered and slipped across the sand and went out from under her. She dropped to her knees with a thump.

Gritting her teeth, she refused to let the mule have his head. Holding on with both hands, she let him drag her, hoping her weight would slow him, eventually managing to quiet the mule.

She heard Tal whisper, "What is it, Ed? What's wrong?"

"Nuthing to worry yourself about, Jones," Crock said, adding a chuckle to his words. "The kid and that big red mule you brought with you just had 'em a little set-to. By Ned, the kid's likely worth his keep. He mighta got hisself a bruise or two, but he won the tussle fair and square."

"Ed, are you . . ."

She looked back at Tal. A pain settled in her chest, ached its way out until it seemed like her whole body hurt. It was getting too dark to see clearly, but she didn't have to see to know what Tal and every other man in the band looked like. They were all bearded, dirty, tattered, forlorn, but Tal—despite his blindness, his shaggy hair, and the tangle of his unkempt beard, was still the handsomest man she had ever seen.

"I'm fine, Mr. Jones. The ravine is right here."

Edwina licked bitter alkali dust off her lips and held back a sigh. Her stomach was threatening to disgrace her. Her mouth was as dry as . . . She couldn't think of a suitable comparison when her mind was focused on the coming gun battle.

As if they were leading her, the mules picked their way into the shelter of the ravine. Edwina helped unharness and picket them before she unsaddled Tal's gelding and cared for him. Then, with Tal standing beside her, she waited silently.

It was full dark before the three scouts, with Case Larson in the lead, came back to the fireless camp Jake had set up in the bottom of the small ravine. Edwina expected to be discovered at any moment, either the outlaws hadn't posted any guards or the rescuers had been lucky.

Traveling in a round about manner, everyone had reached the ravine unscathed. Now, judging by what the scouts had to say, they were less than a quarter of a mile from the box canyon where the outlaws and their captives were located.

"The wagons are in there, and as near we could tell, they ain't been unloaded—except one looks like it's been plundered for a snootful of that rotgut of Raiter's, I'd reckon. The outlaws and the women, if they're still alive, are likely inside the house," Case explained.

"Olivia," Edwina bit back the word that wanted to come out as a moan of despair. Her anger at her sister diminished, but fear was gnawing at her.

Tal eased over and stood a little closer. He didn't say a word, but the gentle squeeze he gave her arm comforted her. Her nieces and their mother were in that canyon, unviolated, waiting and praying for rescue, she told herself fiercely.

The wind had picked up and was beginning to chase the clouds away in small bunches, revealing then quickly hiding the full moon. It showed the stretch of barren, rocky ground they had to traverse to enter the canyon.

"How many of them are in there?" the cook asked one of the scouts. "You have any way of knowing?"

"Nah, there weren't nobody stirring, and all the livestock was in the barn."

"So," Jake said, speaking slowly, "what's the layout look like?"

"It's biggern'n you'd guess from looking at the box canyon."

One of the other scouts added information. "I'd say it looks like it belongs to one of the bigger ranches hereabouts. The house ain't very big, so it's likely a line shack or a bunkhouse. It's well-kept and don't look like no nester's shack, and there's an old barn behind it. And from the looks of it, it'd take dynamite to get them outlaws out of either one iffen that's where they make their stand."

Case said, "That's the truth of it. It ain't gonna be easy, Jake, and it ain't gonna be done quick. I reckon we'd best surprise 'em."

"We'll make less noise if we go in on foot," Jake said. "And I reckon we'd better leave Jones and the kid here to guard the horses and the rest of our supplies."

"Nah," Case said, fairly purring the words, "the kid and his gun go in with the rest of us. Jones can watch the horses."

"Dammit, Case, I told—" Jake started, only to be interrupted by Tal:

"Where Ed goes, I go. That's the straight of it."

"We can hash this out later," Jake said softly, his voice almost lost in the rising wail of the wind. "Right now, we got us some work to do. I, for one, don't intend letting that poor

woman and her daughters spend another day with those outlaws. I'm going in now, even if I have to go alone."

The wind whipped down the ravine. Edwina shivered and
nodded when Jake gave some new orders. She tried to ignore
the weight of the fully loaded six-gun hanging at her hip.

Driven by the capricious wind, clouds tore apart, tattered,
and leaped across the sky. Its light was relentless in its clarity
on the barren earth, turning every clump of sage, every rock,
and every rescuer into a study in silver light and inky shadow.

Against her better judgment, but unable to stop herself,
Edwina moved a half-step closer to Tal. His warmth and
nearness gave her a modicum of comfort.

"It's been a time since they stole the wagons, and they've
likely figured nobody is gonna come out here after 'em. From
the way it looks, they ain't posting no guards. I reckon we'll
all be going in," Jake said, his tone giving the words their full
impact.

No one argued. All the decisions had been made.

There was nothing left for Edwina to do but say a small silent prayer and follow, with Tal's hand on her shoulder,
where Jake Larson led.

The night wasn't full black, but it was a lot darker for him
than it was for the rest of them. Even with Edwina moving
slow and careful in front of him, giving him low-voiced
warning when something was in their path, Tal stumbled
once when they were scrambling up the steep side of the
ravine. Off balance, he rammed into her back, nearly
knocking her flat, but she managed to keep them both on
their feet and moving toward what was going to be one hell of
a fight. Someone was going to get killed.

He had no intention of allowing Edwina to be on the re-
ceiving end of hot lead. Although just how he was going to

prevent it, he didn't have any idea. Dirty-faced, smelling more like mule than a woman, she was grit and stubborn courage right through to her backbone. It was a cinch she wasn't going to do any backing down to save herself.

The lone coyote, if that's what it was and not one of the *tum tum wawas,* howled again. Chills raced each other up his spine. Edwina trembled beneath his hand. Tal squeezed her shoulder, hoping to reassure her.

"There's a wide patch of sharp rocks here. Be careful."

Her whisper jerked him out of his dire thoughts, and he moved closer. It wasn't quiet. Sagebrush rasped and rattled in the wind. Small night creatures scurried and ran: sand trickled down banks. There were other sounds he couldn't put a name to—and each and every one tightened his nerves and honed his worry.

Increasing in fury, the wind tore around them. It was cold, but the chill couldn't hide the strong smell of wood smoke, food cooking, alkali, and sage. The dust and smoke irritated the inside of his nose and Tal couldn't stifle the sneeze that exploded.

Edwina froze in place.

"What the hell was that?" a stranger's voice asked.

"Hell, I dunno. Maybe it was one o'them wild jackasses."

"I don't know. Maybe we ought to check it out. It sounded like somebody sneezing."

"Stop acting like an old woman. You knew what you was getting into when you signed on with this outfit. Grab another keg of that drinking likker and let's go back in where it's warm."

Tal didn't relax until he heard the sound of their retreating footsteps followed by the closing of a door.

"Ed," he whispered, "I can't let—"

"Shhhh!" someone behind them hissed.

Tal couldn't see well, but he knew they were standing, behind a rock that bulked large and dark in front of them. Beyond it the silvery earth faded into shadow except for a few squares of pale-yellowish light that might be the windows in the house, and could see a darker, larger shadow beyond the house. He guessed it was the barn.

Edwina whimpered, "Oh, no."

"What?" he hissed, barely breathing the sound.

"Olivia and the girls. They're taking them out to the barn—"

Before the words were completely out of her mouth, she whirled around, slammed into him, knocked him to the rocky ground, and fell on top of him. A second later, a rifle cracked, sending a bullet to whine past where they lay.

A man grunted and bit off a curse.

Another man, Case by the sound of his voice, whispered, "Jake? Jake? Are you hit?"

In the silence that followed, his voice holding a swelling note of fear, he said "Jake? Dammit, answer me."

Jake, or somebody, coughed and moaned.

Tal shivered and tried to wiggle out from under Edwina and free his Colt at the same time.

Then all hell broke loose.

Between one breath and the next a shooting war had started, and Edwina didn't know who had fired the first shot. She had seen a man with a rifle herding her sister and nieces toward the barn. He had turned and aimed the weapon in their direction. Convinced he could see them and intended to shoot, she had pushed Tal down and now they sprawled behind the meager shelter offered by a rocky outcropping. Tal was trying to get his gun free, but she clung to him and refused to allow him to get himself killed.

Above them bullets whizzed. Zinged. Whined. Crashed into the earth. Thunked into stone. Bored into living flesh. Lead ricocheted in every direction. Rock chips flew.

All around them men swore. Cursed. Cried out.

Both sides fired round after deafening round until she thought she was going to go deaf. But not once did she release her hold on Tal.

It was some time before she realized he was no longer fighting. His arms were around her shaking body, and his hold on her was just as protectively fierce.

Somewhere in their struggles, he had rolled her over. Edwina looked up at his shadowed face, tried to catch her breath, and to still the pounding of her heart. She didn't turn her face away when his came closer until his lips touched hers gently, then with urgent need.

As if to give them the privacy their first kiss required, a cloud covered the moon and plunged the world into darkness. Edwina closed her eyes as the kiss ignited.

Chapter Fifteen

Tal lifted his head but only inches separated their faces. He whispered, "Oh, God," and then the cold rushed back, bringing the fury of the outside world in its wake.

No matter how much she wanted it otherwise, Edwina could only lie there on the cold earth, in the middle of a pitched gun battle, and shiver. Tal said, his deep voice anguished, "I didn't mean to . . . Oh, God, I'm sorry. I had no right to . . ." His voice faded as he eased away from her.

She struggled to a sitting position and huddled against the unyielding comfort of the sheltering stone. Bullets sang lethal songs inches above her head.

When she remembered to breathe, Edwina whispered, "Don't, Tal. Oh, please, don't," not knowing the protest was lost in the booming roar of quickening gunfire. The clouds parted, and the moonlight was bright on both the bunkhouse and the attacking miners. Crocker crawled up to her place of refuge.

She looked at him squarely. "Kid, Jake's been hit. He's back there," the cook pointed to a spot behind them and to his right—"with Case, and Case wants to talk to you."

There was enough light to show the two men. They were lying together in a small depression, Jake on his back and Case on one elbow, leaning over his brother. Despite her fear of the man, she could see that he cared for Jake.

The gunfire was sporadic with more firing from the cabin than from the miners, but it was still loud and deadly. Edwina and Crocker ducked when a bullet grazed the top of the rock, sending out a painful hail of sharp-edged pellets of stone. One grazed Edwina's cheek, and she winced.

Edwina started to crawl in the direction Crocker had indicated. Only then did she realize she had drawn the Colt and was holding it in her shooting hand. Edwina crawled, armed and ready to fire. She wasn't sure who she was going to have to shoot first, Case Larson or the outlaws. She knew Tal was less than a foot behind her when she reached Jake and his brother.

Case said, "We gotta put a end to this pretty damned quick. I've gotta get Jake to a doctor—"

A bullet, sounding as harmless as a buzzing rattlesnake, dug a furrow in the earth just beyond Case's head. He ignored it. "We've gotta smoke them out ta there so Jake can get some doctoring."

Edwina's chin came up. Her eyes narrowed. She was Edwina Parkhurst, and there was work to be done if Olivia was going to get out of that place alive. Edwina was going to do her share of the rescuing.

"Where are we going?" she asked Case.

"No, dammit, you're not going—"

"Yes, Mr. Jones, I am," Edwina said, surprised that her voice was steady. It should have been stark with fear. She took an unsatisfactory breath. It rasped painfully out of her chest. "It's my sister they are trying to rescue. I can't let more men get hurt when . . ." Her voice took on an undertone of pleading, but the need for understanding was directed at him alone. "Mr. Jones, don't you see, I have to do what I can to help?"

Thin, wispy clouds drifted across the moon and dimmed

the light. The world shrunk. For that moment, Talmadge Jones was the only other person who existed in the windswept desolation.

"Yeah, Ed," he said, speaking softly, and as unyielding as ice. "I understand a lot more than you think, that's why I'm going with you."

"No, you ain't going. You're blind as a bat."

Tal laughed. It was soft, low, and cold and it said all that needed saying.

The laugh sent slivers of ice crowding around her heart. The Colt ready in her right hand, she got to her knees and looked at Case.

Case glared at Tal. "Come on, kid, I ain't got time to argue with no damned fool. Iffen he wants to get hisself killed, that's fine. We gotta get around on the far side of that building." He waited until she was on her feet, and then he ran, crouching, taking advantage of every bit of cover, working his way toward the goal.

Edwina was right behind him. She didn't look back to see if Tal was following.

Tal took a deep breath and tried not to think of her soft mouth, the yielding of her body, the woman taste of her. It didn't stop him from cursing himself for being nine kinds of idiot as he followed behind Case and Edwina.

Stumbling into brush, blundering through it, he struggled on. Falling twice, crawling when the lead flew too thick around him, trying to run when he could. He wasn't far behind Edwina when she followed Case to the back of the shack. His breath was coming hard. Sweat all but freezing on his forehead, he stifled a betraying sneeze.

He was there, six-gun drawn, hammer thumbed back, when Case said, "Kid, they got a fire in the stove. I'm gonna boost you up on the roof to plug the top of the stovepipe.

The smoke'll send them out."

"I'm ready."

The moon was drifting down the western sky, leaving Case and Edwina hidden in the shadow of the bunkhouse. Other than their small movements, Tal couldn't see much, but he could hear every sound. The coyotes crying in the distance. The wind whining. The oddly disconnected sounds of Case muttering and Edwina climbing. The indistinguishable murmur of men's voices from inside the building, and the harsh, echoing boom of gunfire.

But what set him on edge, tensed every one of his nerves, was the muffled rasp of disturbed sage brushing across the legs of an approaching man, though he was moving with stealth.

Oooooooooooouuuuuuuuuuuhhhhhh!!!

The howling animal was so close and its cry so unexpected, Tal jumped. It had to be a dog; nothing else would cry like that.

"Son of a bitch."

It was Case who swore, but it wasn't Case firing, hot lead that splatted into the stone of the building close to Tal's right shoulder. It wasn't Case who returned fire—aiming at the spot where the other gun muzzle had flared—and found his mark.

A man screamed in agony and crashed heavily.

"Mr. Jones!" Edwina's frightened cry came from above him.

"I'm fine. Plug the stovepipe and get down quick."

"Moose? You out there? What's going on?" The stranger's low-voiced questions were interrupted by renewed howling from the dog.

Another voice asked, "What the hell's wrong with that damned mutt?"

The dog howled again. Louder.

Tal could hear Edwina mutter something and scrabble around on the roof as he moved closer to Case. "I'll see the kid down. They've figured out what we were trying to do."

Case didn't argue. He just moved over so Tal could position himself beneath Edwina's descending body. She slid off the roof so quickly Tal barely had time to snag her coat, pull her into his arms, and break her fall. He held her for only a second, than released her.

Orange fire burst from the muzzle of Case's revolver. The report was close and loud. A man cried out in pain and Case shouted, "Get down, kid. There's another one of the rotten sons still out there."

Tal didn't have time to straighten out of his stance before one of the miners shouted, "Watch it, boys, they're coming out shooting!"

Case took off toward the barn. He shouted, "Cover me, kid, he's trying to get back into the barn with the women."

Tal heard a door creak open. A woman screamed.

In front of the stone building, a battle raged. It had a full cast of roaring guns, yelling men, and cries of the dying.

Then the gunfire stopped with Crocker's shout, "Case, they're all dead. The line shack smells like a pigsty, but it's warm. You want we should dung it out a mite and move Jake in out of the weather?"

"Yeah."

"Send the kid back up on the roof to unplug that stovepipe."

Case called, "Jones, you hear that?"

Tal drew enough air into his lungs to say, "I heard."

Tal turned her around, stood behind her, and lifted her up, holding her until he was sure she had a good grip on the low roof. Then he waited in the shadow while she scrabbled around on the tarpaper roof and then came skittering over to the edge.

"Mr. Jones? Are you ready? I'm coming down."

Once again she was in his arms briefly, her fingers brushing his cheek in a feathery caress. She whispered, "Thank you," before she stepped out of his arms and moved a few feet away.

"I could see from the roof," she said. Her husky voice shook a little when she whispered, "Crocker has the lantern lit. The outlaws are lying out there. Dead."

He started to reach for her, but she moved another step away. "They killed Charlie, the muleskinner who gave me my coat. I was with him when he died and I—I never saw a man die before. It's easy to write about but, Mr. Jones, how does someone—"

"Kid," he said, hearing someone coming close and not wanting to betray her, "no matter what you do, no matter how ugly it is, you have to go on. You have to live with it even if it cankers your soul. That's about the only choice you have, unless you want to put paid to your own account—and there are those who've done that, too."

"You wouldn't?"

"Not now, but—"

That was all he got out before Crocker, carrying a lantern, came around the corner of the bunkhouse. "You're wanted, kid. There's some real nasty chores that need doing."

Tal hadn't the slightest trouble hearing her sigh. "What do you want me to do this time? Dig graves? Dung out the bunkhouse?"

Crocker sort of chuckled, but it sounded more like nervous laughter than merriment. "Nope, nothing that easy."

"What?"

"Your sister and those girls are in the barn . . ."

"Yes?"

"One of the outlaws is in there with 'em. He's a-threatening to kill 'em all if . . ."

Edwina stopped in front of the cook. Tal was close enough to fight back a little shiver of his own when the dog howled again. "What does Mr. Larson want me to do?"

"Kid, make sure that six-gun of yourn is loaded, 'cause he's a-fixing to send you in after that devil."

Chapter Sixteen

The wind was fierce. Slashing across the high desert, it rattled sagebrush, tore loose weeds and sand and threw them with stinging abandon as thick clouds covered the face of the moon.

The lantern swinging from Crocker's gloved hand threw a meager shaft of yellow light, which did little to battle the immensity of the darkness.

The dog had quit howling, but Edwina didn't need that mournful reminder of her own mortality. She walked beside Crocker on the hoof-churned trail leading from the line shack to the stone barn. Tal walked on her other side.

"Noooo! Don't hurt—"

The plea was just a thread of agonized sound, but Edwina knew who cried. "Becca," she whispered. "It's Becca!"

"Kid," Crocker said, his voice mingling with Tal's.

"Ed, what's wrong? Was that one of the girls?"

"Was what—I didn't hear nothing," Crocker said, sounding aggrieved.

"Yes," she whispered, answering Tal's question and ignoring Crocker. "Oh, hurry, something terrible is—Hurry."

"Mama! Maaaaamaa!"

After the scream there was nothing, not even a whimper of sound coming from structure.

Becca! Edwina had to do something. Dear God, what was

that man doing to Olivia? Why was Becca screaming? Where was Meg?

She reached down and tried to grab the bail of the lantern, but Crocker swung the it out of her reach just as Case snarled from the deep shadow that almost hid the near side of the barn. "Dammit, kid, don't do nothing rash now. We gotta get them outta there safe."

"Yes," she said, not even trying to keep her voice low. "Tell me what to do."

"There's a manure heap, bout half the way down this side and a window where they shoveled dung out the barn. It's not very big, and it's got a shutter on it, but it ain't fastened tight." He hesitated a second. "You go in through that window, whilst I keep that bastard busy up by the front door."

"All right." Even before the words were out of her mouth, Edwina started toward the tiny fingers of light leaking through the crack of the shutter-covered window. She didn't consciously think about it, but she knew Tal was right behind her.

"Kill the bastard if you have to," Case said flatly.

"Yes," she said, meaning it. The Colt was in her hand when she climbed the small, unsteady heap of old horse manure and straw to peek through the narrow crack. Looking in, she tried to locate her sister and the girls.

Tal tugged at her sleeve. She jerked her arm away. The manure pile shifted a little with her sudden movement, throwing her off balance. She grabbed at the barn wall and pushed her face closer to the crack in the shutter.

"Ed?" Tal hissed, his mouth less than an inch from her ear. "What the hell is going on in there?"

It was a drama of life and death lit by a single lantern that trembled in the hand of Edwina's niece, Meg. Her hair lank and straggling down her back, Olivia was on her knees, with her hands folded together in mute supplication. Her head was bowed.

Like a discarded rag doll, Becca sprawled motionless on the dirt floor behind her mother. Meg stood off to one side. Her face was hidden in the shadows, but her head was unbowed and there was a tense watchfulness about her.

The man was a stranger. He was average in height and well into his middle years. In his big hands was a hangman's noose.

"Tell me!" Tal ordered.

"He's—he's . . . Tal, he's going to hang Olivia."

She jerked with all her strength and screamed. "No!" The shutter came loose with a shriek and knocked her into Tal.

Lead whined by above Edwina's head. The Colt bucked in her hand as she returned fire, but her shot went wild.

Case started shooting, shouting, and pounding on the big double doors in the front of the barn.

The lantern in Meg's hand flared high and went out.

Cursing, the madman shot again, aiming toward the dung window. Tal had elbowed Edwina out of the way. He returned fire, shooting toward the muzzle flash of the outlaw's gun. He didn't miss.

And for one horrible moment, Edwina didn't know who he had hit.

Meg screamed, "Mama? Mama, are you hurt?"

A man's deep groan answered.

Edwina took her place beside Tal and tried to see inside the barn. It was black as pitch.

Sounding calm and reassuring, Tal said, "Girl, there's nothing more to be afraid of. We've come to take you back where you belong."

Olivia and the girls were too silent for Edwina's peace of

mind. She pulled her self up into the window opening and started to crawl inside the dark building.

Tal got a good grip on the back of her coat and held her in place. He called to Meg, "Girl, answer me. We're trying to help. Have you got any matches? Can you light the lantern?"

"N-n-nuh, sir," Meg stammered out. "He—he wouldn't let . . ." She sobbed once. "Please, sir, help me. I don't know what to do. Mama won't answer me and he hit Becca . . ."

"Can you walk over to the big doors and lift the bar. There are friends waiting out there. They'll help you."

"I—I . . ."

"Just do it," Tal said gently. "Everything is going to be all right now."

"Yes, sir," the girl answered.

The man's moans probably hadn't kept them from hearing her, but nonetheless Tal shouted, "Case, the man's down, acting like he's dying. One of the girls is going to open the door. Don't shoot her."

"I have to go in. They need me," Edwina whispered.

Tal's breath was warm on her cheek when he responded. "Not yet. The man might be faking it. It won't help anybody if you get yourself killed."

"But, I need to—"

"Wait until Case gives the all-clear and then you can go to your family."

He was telling her a sad farewell. Edwina sighed. Tal tightened his grip on her coat, pulled her a little closer to his warmth and brushed her cold cheek with his lips. For one small instant, Edwina allowed herself to relax, to lean against his broad chest.

One of the big double doors at the front of the barn creaked open, and Crocker's lantern sent in a shaft of light. Case said something soothing to Meg, then went into the barn with Crocker and the lantern.

"He ain't going be doing any shooting anytime soon, less'n it's at Old Nick," Crocker said, holding the lantern high, peering down at the injured man, and then holstering his own gun. "Come on in, Ed, and tell this family of yourn that you're still alive."

The stone wall was thick and the window enclosure deep, but Edwina scrambled across it as soon as Tal released his hold on her coat. Once inside, she turned and said, "Come on. It's only about three feet down to the floor." She held out her hand, but Tal came in without her aid.

The interior of the barn was filled with shadows, and Crocker's lantern did a mad dance every time he moved. What little light there was didn't help Tal. He couldn't see worth a tinker's damn.

One of the girls was crying softly. The other girl wasn't making a sound and that bothered him. He hoped she wasn't hurt badly.

"Olivia, I . . . Are you all right?" Edwina's voice was warm with caring.

Olivia said, without a trace of emotion in her voice, "I don't have a brother."

"Ed here said he was your brother," Crocker answered.

She repeated her earlier statement in the same flat tone. "I don't have a brother."

The man on the floor stopped moaning and said, "He raped her. She was only a little girl. Ambrose Raiter killed her, just as if he strung her up with his own hand."

Case ignored the man to ask Olivia, "What did the kid do, ma'am, run off when there was trouble? Is that why you're disowning him, because you're thinking he's a coward?"

She didn't answer him.

Her silence didn't stop Case. He continued, "I knew the little devil was hiding something. Well, it ain't hid no more. Now, everbody's gonna know just what kind-a yellow-bellied rat he is. Ain't that right, kid?" He laughed.

Crocker interrupted. "That varmit is gut-shot and he's gonna be cashing in his chips soon. Ma'am, I don't reckon you and the girls want to stay in here and listen to that kind of filthy talk. Why don't we take you up to the line shack and let you get warm. Jake and a couple of others took some lead and a woman's hand would be welcome in the—"

"I got him back," the dying man said. "Took his wife just like he did my daughter. Now, I'm gonna string her up, just like—" He coughed and was silent.

"Olivia, I know you don't like what I did, but does it matter so much now? Can't you forget about my sins long enough to let me—Oh, please, tell me, are you hurt bad?"

Olivia ignored her and spoke to Crocker, "Yes, I'd like very much to leave here. I know he's dying, but I can't stop hating—I know it's my Christian duty to pray for his soul, but, may God forgive me, I can't."

"No, ma'am," Crocker said, "I don't reckon you can."

Tal listened as they sorted themselves out. "Kid," Case said as they were leaving, "you better go down to the other camp with one of the boys and bring back the cart and the animals. Take Jones with you when you go. He's a good shot for a blind man, and whilst I don't reckon you need him, it pays to be careful."

"Yes, sir," Edwina said.

It was late before they got the cart to the bunkhouse, the mules and horses in the barn, and the bedrolls sorted out. While they were gone, the bunkhouse had been given a hasty cleaning, food had been cooked, and the injured men had received some doctoring. Olivia was assisting with the nursing, and Jake sounded pleased with the tending she was giving him.

Case walked over to where Tal was standing by the wall, eating ham and corn pone out of a tin plate. "Come morning, Jake's gonna send a couple of the boys to Raiter's place to tell him what happened here."

Tal nodded, but he wondered why Case was confiding in him. While he waited, Tal kept on eating, chewing every bite, and tasting nothing. The room was dimly lit, too shadowy for him to see much, but it was almost warm. He liked that, even if he didn't like the acrid taint of smoke that still lingered, mixing with the ranker smells of sweat, blood, and medicine.

Case cleared his throat. "I know it ain't warm out there but considering the way Miz Raiter is feeling about the kid, you and the kid oughta sleep out in the barn."

Tal didn't want to spend the night alone in the barn with Edwina.

"It ain't too easy on the kid, neither, Jones. I don't think he'd want to rile his sister anymore. Maybe if I tell Miz Raiter about today, she won't go on thinking he's a coward."

"Maybe." Tal knew more about what had happened between the sisters than Case did, and he wasn't able to understand Olivia's attitude.

"You'll do it, then?"

"I suppose."

"Thanks, Jones."

Tal was tired and still chilled, but none of that mattered.

"I'll go tell the kid," Case said.

"God help me," Tal muttered. He emptied the plate, eased over and placed it on the table, and waited for Edwina.

Chapter Seventeen

Trying not to breathe too deeply, Edwina pulled her coat more tightly around her. The miners had done a less than thorough job of cleaning the line shack.

It was perhaps twenty-five feet long and ten feet wide, and nothing more than low stone walls with a roof of rough boards nailed onto rafters of peeled poles. Part of the interior had been pasted over with yellowed, rodent-gnawed newspapers. The two small window holes, now covered with blankets, had never seen a pane of glass. The floor was hard-packed dirt under an accumulation of filth.

One end of the room was devoted to sleeping, with built-in bunks of rough planks, stacked three high, on both sides. The other end held an iron stove for cooking and warmth and a battered table with benches. Beyond some whiskey kegs scattered around for seating and some cupboards above a dry sink, that was the sum total of the furnishings. Even with four lanterns lit, it was still dark and gloomy. The stench of whiskey, sweat, urine, vomit, blood, and death was pervasive.

One of the rescue party had been killed, three others wounded, but none as seriously as Jake. Judging from their current conversation, the survivors were jubilant because the outlaws were dead. According to the miners, it was justice that the bodies of the outlaws were out in the dark and covered with a tarp until they could be buried in the morning.

Knowing what they had done to the muleskinners and her own family, Edwina wasn't sorry the men were dead. She was so tired her legs would hardly hold her. She ached all over and was so dirty she doubted that she'd ever come clean.

Stomach churning, palms sweating, Edwina hovered near Jake Larson's bunk. He appeared to be resting comfortably after a rough surgery. One of the miners had cut a bullet from his thigh and cauterized the wound with whiskey and a red-hot stove poker. It wasn't Jake that held her attention; it was Olivia. *She* wiped Jake's face with a damp cloth, answered his questions softly, and acted as if Edwina didn't exist.

"Lobo Chance, that writer feller, was he captured with you?" Jake asked. His voice was soft, and he was watching Olivia as if she were an angel.

"No," she answered.

Jake took in a quick breath. "But he was traveling with you, wasn't he, ma'am? On one of the wagons maybe?"

Edwina waited. She was sure Olivia was going to reveal her secret. She hoped her sister would acknowledge her that much, but it didn't happen.

"I heard that was true, Mr. Larson," Olivia said. "You'd better try to get some rest."

Jake closed his eyes and then opened them. "You'll not leave?"

Olivia smiled thinly. "I'll stay right here."

Not once during the exchange did Olivia glance in Edwina's direction. Edwina couldn't deny the hurt that was swelling inside her chest and trying to turn itself into a torrent of tears.

Case interrupted her chaotic thoughts. "Kid," he said, grabbing one of the lanterns near where she was standing. "There's been a lot of talk about them Indians being off the reservation and the hell they're raising. Likely it's true, but, kid, we ain't seen hide nor hair of no Paiutes since we left Idaho. So I reckon we ain't in any danger from Indians, but some of them damned outlaws might have got away in the confusion."

He looked toward his brother and then toward the end bunk where the two girls were sleeping. He grinned. It was nothing more than a flash of teeth within the tangle of his beard. "That sister of yours is mad at you right now, but she'll still need protecting just the same."

Not sure where the conversation was heading but in agreement so far, she nodded.

"I've got lookouts posted on the canyon walls, but they ain't gonna be able to see everything, so I want you and Jones to guard the barn. Truth to tell, I don't reckon it needs much guarding but I'd feel easier in my mind if it was."

He clapped her on the shoulder. "Don't worry about it none. You did good today, better than many a man would, and I reckon your sister will see what you did for her and come around sooner or later. When it comes right down to it, kin is kin. And she knows it."

Even though she was sure Olivia wasn't going to come around or forgive, Edwina nodded again.

He handed her the lantern. "You'll be needing this. Jones is waiting by the door. Your gear's there with him."

Grabbing the chance to get out of the line shack, she did as she was told. Tal had his bedroll on his shoulder, his possible bag—with the wooden box of handwritten manuscripts for their dime novels hidden inside—in his hand.

There was no need to speak. Bending to pick up her own bedroll, Edwina looked back to where her sister stood and watched as Case brought over a whiskey barrel for Olivia to sit on at Jake's side. Olivia smiled at the younger Larson and thanked him. She did not acknowledge Edwina's existence. It wasn't far to the barn, but it was cold. The wind was icy and Edwina's teeth were chattering before she pushed the barn door open. "We're here."

She stood aside so Tal could enter, then followed. Closing the door behind them and dropping the bar in place, Edwina held the lantern high and surveyed the barn. She deliberately kept away all thoughts of the man who had died there. She felt no pity for him and no forgiveness for what he had done to her sister. *Olivia.* Edwina sighed before she turned her attention back to finding them a place to sleep.

The barn was large with box stalls down one side and a series of ropes forming a temporary pen strung down the other. Nose-burning ripe with animal odors, the big stone structure was full to capacity. Their own mounts and draft mules were crowded in with the mules and horses of the outlaws. The horses were bedded down two to a stall, with the mules all herded together behind the ropes of the corral, leaving a small center aisle clear of the animals.

"Mr. Jones," she said, hating the tremor in her voice. Determined to master herself, Edwina tried again. "Mr. Jones, there's not a whole lot of room left, but—"

"Anyplace will do," he said gruffly.

Something was troubling him, she guessed from his attitude. She wanted to ask what was wrong, but fighting her own dark thoughts was all she could manage at the moment. Tired beyond belief, she wanted nothing more than to lie down and sleep. And not shed the hot tears that fought to be released.

Just beyond the pool of light cast by the lantern, eerie shadows wavered. She led Tal through the barn to a rickety ladder on the back wall. It was a few splintery slats pegged to poles standing upright and flat against the stone wall, making it possible to gain access to a small hayloft that extended into the barn ten or twelve feet above the floor. It afforded them the only clear spot to toss down their bedrolls.

As silent as he was, her fingers barely plucking at his coat, she led him to the ladder and started him on his climb with nothing more than a warning that the crossbars were far apart. Following him up to the platform, she hung the lantern on a peg and spread a thick layer of the dried grass on the floor.

Edwina made short work of the bedrolls. Within minutes, they were laid out side by side, taking up most of the space that wasn't being used to store hay. After Tal had collapsed on his, Edwina extinguished the light.

Knowing he couldn't see them, but nonetheless thankful for the darkness that hide her tears, she made her way to her pallet. Placing the loaded six-gun within easy reach, Edwina pulled off her boots and coat and slid under the covers.

Some warmth might be coming up from the animals below, but Edwina couldn't feel it. The hay that should have given softness and warmth to her bed developed lumps that poked at her. She couldn't force her weary limbs to relax or find the sleep that eluded her. And she couldn't stop the tears.

Outside, the dog howled again. The sound came low and mournful through the stone of the walls. As if in answer to the cry, Edwina's sobs broke free. Her hands covered her mouth.

"What? Dammit, Ed, what . . . ? Are you hurt?" It was an urgent question. He crawled out of his bed and kneeled at her side. Fumbling in the darkness, his hands brushed her face and came back to trace its outline. His thumbs wiped away her tears before he slid an arm beneath her shaking shoulders and lifted her up. One hand patting her back, he cradled her.

Edwina didn't cry easily. Each sob clawed at the lining of her throat, wild and fierce. Only Tal's encircling arms offered any comfort. His arms tightened and pulled her close against his pounding heart. For an instant she tried to resist, but his warmth was irresistible. Edwina relaxed into his embrace, raised her tear-wet face, and whispered, "Oh, Tal, Olivia will never forgive me. My own sister, she looked right at me and denied I even existed. And the girls, too."

Whatever he might have been thinking, he didn't say a word about her sister's ungratefulness. Talmadge Jones just rocked Edwina gently and whispered, "Shhh, sweetheart. Just rest. It doesn't matter."

Edwina swallowed a sob and hiccuped.

His hold tightened; his voice roughened. "Don't, love, don't. You did what you had to do. Right or wrong, there's no going back to change it."

His cheek against her hair, he rocked her like a babe, but she didn't feel like a child. She felt like a woman. "Oh, Tal," she whispered.

"Edwina?"

He was questioning, and Edwina was confused until he bent his head, touched his cold lips to her salty ones, and kissed her. It held a hint of passion, but it was a gentle loving kiss. Untutored in the ways of woman and man, but eager to respond to his touch, her lips softened of their own accord, parted slightly, and Edwina returned the kiss threatening to consume her.

Her arms encircled his neck and drew him closer. The kiss deepened, but only for a brief enchanted moment. It was a lovers' moment that existed outside of time and beyond responsibility. Then Tal lifted his head and left coldness where his lips had been.

He drew in a breath. She could feel him shake as it expanded his chest. "Edwina," he said, "I would give my soul to . . . But, I can't." He held her close for a moment longer before he eased her back onto her narrow bed and released her.

"No," Edwina whispered hoarsely. "Don't. I want you to—"

Pulling the covers snugly around her, he touched her face with gentle fingers. "I love you," he said slowly.

In the silence that followed, she asked, "Why then, can't you—?"

"I'm not like your family, Edwina I can't take everything from you and give nothing in return."

"I know that," she said. "But I don't see why . . ."

Somewhere in the darkness on the barn floor, something moved. A horse whickered and a mule squealed. Something crashed.

Edwina stiffened, listening intently. Other than the slither of scurrying rodents, quiet claimed the barn.

Tal leaned down and kissed her on the forehead. "Edwina," he said, "I can't leave you with more responsibility, or take what's left of your good name."

"My good name," she snorted, trying to hide the hurt his words caused her. "I don't have a good name, or, at least, I won't have after Olivia gets to Mother and the preacher. She'll make sure everyone knows that not only am I Lobo Chance, but that I spent many nights alone with a man."

He put his finger on her lips, stopping her words. "Possibly she will. And that's going to hurt you, but would it make it better for you if I got you with child?" he asked softly.

"Dear God," she said, "I didn't think. Oh, Tal, I . . ." Fire burned her face and she wished that she could die from shame. A child? She had never thought beyond the moment.

"I wish it could be different," Tal said.

"But it can't, can it?" Edwina asked, wanting him to say, "Yes, it can. We love each other. We will find a way."

He didn't. He just touched his finger to her lips again,

leaving a warm tingle. "I'm sorry, Edwina. I should never have kissed you."

"I'm glad you did," Edwina said. The memory of those two kisses would have to last her for the rest of her life. She would treasure them.

Tal eased back on his heels, but he didn't leave her side.

"It's cold. Better get back in bed," she suggested, her voice full of weariness.

Love and desire tangled inside him, he needed the cold. In fact, he needed to be dunked in a horse trough of icy water, although even that wouldn't quench the fire that just thinking about Edwina kindled in him.

"Go to sleep," he said softly. "Maybe we . . . Ah, hell, talking's not going to change a damned thing."

"I know," she said, her voice barely audible. She sobbed again.

This time, she wasn't crying for a selfish sister. She was crying for him. He reached for her. It wasn't strength of character that stopped him.

Screech!

Tal recognized the sound. He knew the shutter on the dung window was being pried loose. Turning to his pallet, he found his gun.

"What?"

"Shhh! Somebody's trying to climb in the window."

Hay rustled. He thought she was getting her own six-shooter.

"Tal," she said, crawling over until she was touching him. Her warm breath tickled his ear as she whispered, "The platform we're on doesn't have a railing or anything. Be careful."

Horses snorted. A mule squealed. The shutter squalled again. A male voice muttered, "Blast it."

Tal thought he could see a faint outline of paler dark

where the window should be. It was a pale rectangle with a darker patch in the middle.

He cocked the Colt, pointed it toward the paleness. "Come on in, stranger," he said quietly, "if you want to get your head blown off."

The silence stretched. Tal could feel sweat slicking the palm of his hand as his finger tightened on the trigger. Beside him he heard the click as Edwina cocked her own six-gun.

Chapter Eighteen

Weariness sapped her strength. Her swollen eyes burned, but her arms were steady. It took both of her weather-chapped hands to hold the heavy six-gun, but her aim never wavered. The Colt was cocked. Her forefinger was snug around the trigger. The darker shadow in the middle of the dung window was her target. All she needed was for the shadow to move. Or for Tal to give the word.

Tal spoke calm and deadly "Come on in, stranger, if you don't mind having a hole blown through you."

"Tarnation, Jones, don't shoot!" a man yelled. He sounded frightened. "It's me, Crocker."

He mumbled on, then mustered enough sense to ask, "You ain't gonna shoot me, are you? Kid, tell him. I ain't aiming to hurt nobody. I just had me a drink or two of that whiskey. Tell him, kid."

"Tal?"

He sighed. "Better light the lantern and go get him. Likely he's too drunk to climb up by himself."

"Yes," she said. Edwina wanted to touch Tal and to tell him she understood, but there was no time for that. She lit the lantern, pulled on her boots and coat, and started toward the rickety ladder.

Tal stopped her. "Take your gun."

Listening with half an ear to the sounds from the barn

170

floor, she found the gun belt, strapped it on, and made sure the Colt was snug in the holster. The animals were moving restlessly. Crocker was swearing and, judging by the noise he was making, he had already fallen through the dung door and was in danger of being stepped on by the mules. It was time to go fish him out of the corral and try to get him up to the loft.

"Be careful," Tal said, his voice a growly whisper. His hand reached out and his fingers barely brushed her cheek.

"I'll be careful," she managed to say as she started to climb down to rescue Crocker. They had accepted the only future that was open to them. That much was true, but Edwina was aware that she wasn't any happier than Tal.

Sprawled where he had landed, looking up at the lantern, Crocker smiled and mumbled, "I reckon you got here just in time, kid. That there big red mule was fixing to take a bite outta my hide. Swear he was."

In no mood to deal with the cook's drunken foolishness, she forced him up and sent him staggering toward the ladder, his bedroll drooping from his shoulder and a ribald song dribbling from his lips.

By the time she boosted him up to the loft and got him bedded down, Edwina was so tired that she wasn't sure she could make it to her own bedroll. Taking a deep breath, she blew out the lantern and stood there.

"Kid? You all right?" Tal asked.

Not about to add to his worry, she responded quickly, "Yes, I was catching my breath." She was crawling into her bed when Crocker mumbled.

"Ya know. I'm thinking old Jake is smitten with that sister of yours, kid. Too bad she's that Raiter's wife. Jake's a good man. He'd treat her decent like. I reckon Raiter ain't gonna do that, is he?"

"No, I don't suppose he will," Edwina said. Raiter had

never once treated Olivia with any degree of respect. The man was a beast with no decency in him. She sighed, but it was only partly for her sister.

"There's divorce. You don't reckon she . . . ? Nah, she wouldn't. God-fearing women figger that's a going-to-hell sin for sure."

"Go to sleep," Tal snapped.

"Yes, sir, Mr. Jones," Crocker said, adding a snicker. "I reckon we all need our rest iffen we're gonna be pulling out tomorrow."

"Tomorrow?" Tal asked. "Is Jake up to traveling that soon?"

The only answer he got from Crocker was a loud snore, one that called forth new restlessness from the animals. Tal poked the man, ordered him to turn over.

Quiet followed, but Edwina was a long time finding sleep.

Crocker's renewed snoring brought her awake, still dirty, warm, and wanting. Sighing, she turned to her side and pulled the covers over her head. She managed to fall asleep again, but there was no rest in it. And no joy.

The dead outlaws were stacked beneath a bank and covered over with a layer of alkali and sand. To protect them from desecration by animals, rocks were piled on the communal grave. The dead miner was buried separately and with more respect.

After the burying, where Olivia asked God to forgive the outlaws their sins, Case tossed Edwina a sweat-stained hat. "Here, kid. It ain't much, but it'll keep your head warm while you're driving a team of mules to Raiter's saloon and crib."

She wanted a hat for more than the warmth it offered, but she looked at the object in her hands with a dubious eye. Not because it belonged to a dead man, but because of the small visitors it might harbor.

Seeing her expression, Case laughed. "Hell," he said, "it's too damned cold for lice. Wear it. I got another one for Jones."

"Thanks," she said, touched by the act of kindness, but still wary of the man himself.

"See to rigging one of them whiskey wagons for the women and Jake to ride in."

"Yes, sir," she said, jamming the hat down on her head and heading toward the wagons.

"Me'n the boys'll move the whiskey, rig up some bows, and spread the canvas. I reckon you'd better take Crocker and haul a bunch of hay up here. Them wagons will need some padding."

Within minutes, Crocker, complaining of a headache and smelling of strong drink, joined her. "Hair of the dog," he growled, taking another from his canteen. "Keeps the cold out. God, kid, I hate that damned wind. I gotta get a little rest." He staggered off toward the back of the barn. It wasn't long until his snores were loud enough to rattle the beams.

Working without him, Edwina was carrying a forkful of hay out the barn door when she caught a glimpse of blue. Heart thudding, she set the pitchfork down and eased the six-shooter out of the holster. It didn't take long to discover the person in blue wasn't a threat. Edwina eased Colt back into the holster, but she didn't stop walking until she was less than a yard from the girl who was kneeling beside a skinny, yellowish dog. She crooned to the beast as she fed it table scraps from the filled plate she held in her left hand.

The sun was at Edwina's back, sending her shadow before her. Before it touched the girl, Edwina stopped and tried to clear her throat. It was a small sound, almost hidden in the keening of the wind, but it should have been heard. However, neither child nor dog seemed aware that she was standing there.

Dressed in a thick wool cloak, its hood fallen back to let the sun touch her hair, Becca looked different than she had the day before. Her hair, while it was still dirty, had been brushed, plaited, and tied with blue ribbons. Hanging below the cloak, dragging on the sandy earth, was a length of clean but wrinkled skirt—most certainly from Olivia's trunks Jake had insisted they bring with them.

"Becca, honey, are you—" The soft words were out before Edwina could close her mouth. The wind sent icy fingers to lift the short hair on Edwina's neck, billow the child's blue skirt, and whip the dog with a spray of sand. He winced, but kept on gobbling the breakfast leftovers Becca gave him.

Sounding defensive, Becca turned her head and looked up at Edwina. Her soft lower lip trembling, she said, "Mr. Jake said I could feed the dog. He—he's hungry. He belonged to the old man who was here. They shot him." Tears filled her eyes. She didn't try to wipe them away. She knelt there, holding the plate, crying silently.

"Oh, sweetheart, I'm so sorry." Stepping forward, she wanted to comfort her niece.

It didn't happen.

His neck hair standing up, the dog growled, showing large, sharp teeth and serious intent to do Edwina bodily harm.

Becca stood, put her hand on the dog's shoulder, and lifted her chin. "Please excuse us, sir. My mother doesn't allow me to talk to strangers."

The girl's words hurt. Feeling as if she had been kicked in the chest by one of the mules, Edwina couldn't answer. Rejected by everyone she knew and loved, Edwina muttered, "Yes, of course," and turned and walked back to the barn.

★ ★ ★ ★ ★

Slumped at the table in the line shack, Tal thought about Edwina. He had sworn to get her off the high desert and that was going to happen very soon. In a couple of days, if the miner was right when he said that was the time it took to travel to Raiter's.

He pondered the next problem. When she got there, what was going to happen? She could telegraph her publisher and tell him Lobo Chance was safe and had enough written to almost fulfill the contract. Then what? Edwina would just have to catch the stage and go home. If she had a home after Olivia finished her tale-bearing and judging.

A hand fell on his shoulder and shook him. "Jones, I need to talk to you private. Come outside."

He recognized Case Larson's voice and that the other man needed to talk to him about something serious. He stood, picked up the hat Case had given him earlier. "Lead the way."

He followed Case out into sun bright enough to make him blink and narrow his eyes to slits. He could see fairly well in the light and less well inside buildings. He thought he was going to get most of his sight back in one eye, but the other didn't seem near as promising. When this was over, he could go south and find a job sheepherding. He wasn't going to be a gunfighter again and the knowledge didn't cause him any sorrow.

Edwina was by the wagons, helping one of the miners tie a tarp over the whiskey barrels. He couldn't see her plainly.

Case walked on until they were well away from the line shack before he turned to Tal. " 'Pears like you can see a mite now. Jones, I'm in a hell of a fix. Jake is determined to send a couple of the men ahead to tell Raiter what happened to his wife.

175

"Jake's thinking that'll ease it some for Miz Raiter when she has to face him. I ain't so sure he oughta be told a damned thing. It was his filthy doings with that girl what got his wife hurt."

Tal nodded agreement and waited for the younger Larson to explain what was troubling him.

Case leaned over, pulled something off a bush, and crumbled it between his fingers, releasing the pungent odor of sage. Dropping it to the sandy earth, he looked at Tal, considering his words carefully before he spoke.

Case's face was a blur, dark on the bottom where his whiskers were, lighter around his eyes, but Tal looked at him straight. "If you're planning on sending me and the kid, you'd better make other plans."

"Dammit, man, I ain't—"

"The kid is not going to Raiter and tell him Olivia was raped."

"You could—"

"No. Where Ed is, I stay."

"But—"

"No."

The wind rattled sagebrush and tugged at his hat, but Tal stood there, feet apart, thumb hooked on his gun belt. He stared at the other man until Case looked away.

"I reckon you're right," Case said finally. "It wouldn't be fitting. I'll send somebody else, but who in hell is going to drive Raiter's whiskey wagons? The kid is the only one who knows a hill of beans about mules."

He didn't like mules, but the thought of being alone with Edwina disturbed him more than driving a whole herd of the cantankerous beasts. It wasn't what he wanted to say, but he said, "If somebody can hitch 'em up, I'll drive one of the wagons."

He could almost hear Case cogitating. "We can leave the cart here," he said. "Double up the whiskey wagons so's we only need two. That way, Crocker can drive one and the kid one. We can put the tamest mules on Jake's wagon and let you drive that." He pinched off some more sage and held it while he looked up at the sky and then at the ground.

"Jones, it'll have to be the lead wagon because the ladies and Jake don't need to be eating dust all the way. I reckon you can't see enough to—"

"Me or one of the other boys can ride alongside your mules, keep you pointed in the right direction. Then, I reckon, if we can keep him sober long enough, Crocker can drive the second wagon. The kid can handle the last one. That suit you?"

Licking alkali dust off his lips, Tal fingered his mustache, momentarily regretting it was so overgrown, and nodded.

Before Tal could comment, Case walked away, clearly intent on setting his plan in motion, and getting them on the road before too much time had passed. He was nearly at the wagons, already giving orders, before Tal started back to where the miners and Edwina labored. They were moving heavy kegs of whiskey from one wagon to another.

He hadn't yet seen her face, but he knew the high cheekbones were hidden under a layer of dirt. Her generous mouth was cracked from the weather. Her fine eyes were red with weeping. She was tall, slim, and beautiful. Edwina Parkhurst was everything he'd ever wanted in a friend, a love, and a woman. She was courage, grace, compassion, and too damned good for him.

One of the miners, he thought it was Milch but wasn't sure, laughed, sounding out of breath and out of sorts "These barrels are damned heavy. It's a good thing them outlaws was drinking men. They musta swilled down more'n their share of this drinking whiskey. And, I don't mind telling ya that I'm glad they did. Otherwise we wouldn't have a prayer of doing this."

Someone else laughed low and agreed.

A third man said, "Hell, we're doing Raiter the favor. Maybe we oughta be sampling a bit more of this rotgut our ownselfs. What'ya say, Case? This is damned hot work for such a cold day. Likely as not our sweat's gonna freeze solid and turn us . . ."

Ignoring their banter, Tal walked a little faster when he heard Edwina's husky voice ask, "What's in these boxes, Mr. Larson? Are we supposed to move them also?"

The side of the freight wagon was splintered and rough under his hand, and Tal was standing close beside Edwina when Case looked down into the nearly empty wagon bed. "That filthy son-of-a-bitch," Larson snarled. "He ought to be strung up for pulling a trick like this."

"Who? What is it? What's the matter?" Edwina asked.

Tal didn't have to ask what she had found. He couldn't see well enough to read what was printed on the long wooden boxes, but he didn't have to. He had smelled that odor before. *And he had dealt in the death that followed in its wake.*

Chapter Nineteen

Unable to understand the commotion, Edwina looked at the boxes of rifles and then at Tal. "What is it?" she asked again. "What's wrong?"

It wasn't Tal that answered, but he did move a step in her direction.

"Indians," Case snapped, glaring at the wooden boxes. "Indians and Raiter."

Indians? Her heart hammering, she looked around, expecting to see hordes of painted warriors streaming in from all sides. There was nothing out of the ordinary in the monotone depths of the canyon. A guard stood on one of the high walls to the north, and there was another guard on the south wall. Cold light and little comfort, the winter sun was nearing the top of the sky. The bank of clouds in the west was building dark and ominous, threatening a new storm.

The icy wind changed directions and threw sand and alkali in her face. Wiping it away with the back of her hand, Edwina looked at the boxes. "Indians and Ambrose? Mr. Larson, I don't understand what you're implying."

"You ain't that big a fool," Case snapped, shifting his narrow gaze upon her.

Evidently Tal had doubts about the man's intent. His hand not far from his Colt, he took a step toward Case.

One of the miners muttered, "Case, you gotta short fuse

these days. The kid ain't nothing but a tenderfoot. Whatever it is that's going on here ain't none of his doing."

"Kid," Milch explained, "what Case there is saying is that Raiter's got way too many guns here. From the looks of it, he might be fixing to sell them to the Indians."

Nothing Ambrose Raiter could do would surprise her. However, she tried to give him the benefit of the doubt. The men were making a judgment on flimsy evidence, but they knew a lot more about the West than she did. If Ambrose was really planning on selling guns to the Indians, he would have to be stopped before more innocent people were killed.

"That's terrible. Do we have to take them to him? I mean, can't you just throw them away, or hide them here, or—"

She stopped when she realized the miners were looking at her and shaking their heads, not as if they had discovered her secret, but acting like she wanted them to commit a crime.

No one said anything until Case turned to look down canyon. He cleared his throat, took off his battered hat, beat some of the dust out of it against his leg, clapped it back on his head, and finally said, "I don't know where you got a damn fool idea like that, but we ain't thieves, kid."

He sounded insulted, but his words were making no sense. After all, she had only said they should get rid of the guns, she hadn't asked them to steal anything. "What does that mean?"

"They're Raiter's property," a miner standing behind her said slowly.

"But if Ambrose is going to sell—"

Case shook his head.

She tried again. "We could unload them. Hide them in the barn. If they're his, let him come—"

"Yeah, I reckon we could," Milch said, "but this is Injun country."

They continued to argue. It got louder and more profane until Olivia came out of the line shack. Her black serge skirts billowed in the wind, giving a quick glimpse of wrinkled petticoats. A black shawl covering her head and held tight around narrow shoulders, she stopped a dozen feet away.

Edwina looked at her sister and forgot her own hurt. Wanting nothing more than to go to her and offer comfort, but not daring, she just stood there, aching for every mark on her sister's thin face. A bruise purpled one cheekbone. The other one was cut and forming a scab. One of her eyes was blackened and swollen and both had dark circles beneath them. Her lower lip was split, and another bruise marred the skin of her jaw.

"Dear God," Edwina whispered, seeing Olivia for the first time in full light. She swallowed hard and lifted her hands in silent entreaty. She let them fall when Olivia ignored her completely.

Looking at the dusty group of men, Olivia clasped her hands in front of her bosom, and said, not loudly, "Gentlemen, please."

The quarreling stopped instantly. Three or four of the bearded men looked down at the ground and shuffled their worn boots in the sandy earth. One mumbled a quick apology.

After a second or two, Case said, "Miz Raiter, we was just . . . There's rifles in the wagons and—"

"Yes," Olivia said, swallowing rather quickly. She stood a little straighter and licked her lips. "My girls are in tears. The arguing is frightening them."

"Ma'am," Milch said, whipping off his hat and holding it against his chest. "I'm real sorry. Why, we wouldn't hurt them purty little girls for nothing."

Olivia found nothing amusing in the man's discomfort.

181

Looking at Case, she took a quick breath. "Your brother wants to see you."

Case was across the space that separated them and at her side between one breath and the next. He spoke to her quietly and offered his arm. Olivia took it, allowed him to lead her back into the line shack. Not once did she acknowledge Edwina's presence.

"Poor Livy," she whispered.

Perhaps Tal was the only one who heard. At any rate, he was the only one who answered. He said, sounding almost as sad as Edwina was feeling, he said, "She'll be a long time healing."

That thought repeated itself over and over as Edwina helped load the rifles into the other wagons. The rifles belonged to Ambrose, the same as Olivia and the girls did. They were all his lawful possessions.

Shivering, Tal huddled deeper into his slicker. The force of the wind had lessened, but the icy pellets of snow were falling more thickly. The reins in his hands were stiff with cold, but the mules pulling the lead wagon—the four he'd been driving since they left the canyon the day before—were plodding steadily toward the raw little town where Raiter had his saloon.

Shaking loose the snow that had settled in his beard, he covered one eye with his palm. That way, he could see well enough to know they were traveling north and east and approaching another range of hills. The sagebrush and rabbit grass were dark against the snowy ground, and he could see the darker forms of stunted junipers and outcroppings of stone.

"Hush, girls," Olivia said. "Mr. Larson is sleeping and I don't want . . ."

The girls, Meg and Becca, continued their nattering and whining, bickering and complaining. "I'm cold, Mama," the littler one said.

"I know, dear. Put another quilt around you and snuggle down with your sister," Olivia answered. "And, dear, make your dog lie down."

"You don't—" Becca started to cry.

Meg said, "I don't know why Mama let you bring him, Becca. It's just silly, when you know you won't be allowed to keep him."

"I will, too."

"Please, Becca, don't. Your father doesn't like house pets."

"It doesn't matter," Becca insisted. "Mr. Case said he would take care of him for me."

The snowstorm worsened. The wind howled.

Case eased his horse back from the head of the mule team to announce, "We'll be there within the hour. I reckon everybody will be thankful to have a hot meal in their bellies and someplace to bed down out of this cold."

Amen to that, Tal thought. Warm and dry sounded good. He hunched a little deeper into the meager warmth of the slicker and sighed. He was old enough to know better, but he was still lovesick. The way he was feeling, he'd be better off to shoot himself and be done with it.

It didn't sweeten his mood any to hear Jake speaking to Olivia, "I wish we could found that Lobo Chance fella."

"I found Lobo Chance," Tal muttered quietly. "Rather, Chance found me, loaded me into a buggy, dosed me with pain killer, and saved my miserable life."

It was well over an hour before Edwina's team of weary mules crested a final hill and started down the winding track that led into the backside of the pitiful sprawl of buildings that was trying to pass as a growing town. Although it was not long after noon, the sun was invisible in the gray of the overcast sky. Both the wind and the snow had died to a sporadic gust or an errant flurry.

Coming into Raiter's town, whatever its name was, meant only that she would be saying good-bye to Tal and hello to hell. That's what Edwina's life was going to be. She knew it was a hell of her own making. Still, if she had the power, she wouldn't go back and change what she had done. Her family had needed food and shelter; she had given them that. She'd done the same for Olivia and the girls. She had done the only thing she knew how to do, and now she was going to lose that family. She was going to be damned to hell in the bargain—a hell that had no tall, broad-shouldered, amber-eyed gunfighter. Well, she had a little time. Olivia wasn't going to be able to talk to their mother soon, unless she sent a telegram.

The off-front mule stumbled and almost went down. Edwina shouted encouragement. Throwing her weight on the hand brake, she slowed the heavy wagon until the mule regained his footing. The rest of the team, sensing the end of their journey was in sight, tugged at the harness. Hauling back on the lines, she managed to control them, but she was sweating before they acknowledged her leadership.

The mules were stepping high after they forded a shallow, ice-rimmed creek and headed into town. They passed a hotel so new its paint still smelled and a laundry carrying a crudely lettered sign announcing hot baths for two-bits. Boardwalks on both sides of the street offered foot traffic a degree of comfort and safety.

The other wagons had already come to a halt across the rutted street from a two-story frame building which boasted a garish sign proclaiming it to be the Wild Horse Saloon, A.

Raiter, Prop. Two women with hooded cloaks clutched around them hurried down the boardwalk. They were coming from the direction of the hotel and heading toward the wagons.

A man came up beside the wagon and spat out a stream of brown tobacco juice. "Mr. Raiter said fer y'all to leave them wagons right here. He aims to look them over before giving out any rewards.

"Right now, I'm gonna unhitch the mules and take 'em over to the livery barn." He pointed down the street, in the general direction of a large structure with a corral behind it.

Nodding, she set the brake and climbed down from the wagon seat. Stretching, trying to twist some of the stiffness out of her abused body, Edwina was standing on the board-walk when the older women approached. The wind chose that moment to whip back one woman's hood and reveal her face. There were tears running down her pale cheeks and she cried, "Oh, thank the Good Lord, you're safe, daughter." Arms out-stretched, reaching, she ran toward Edwina.

Stunned by her sudden appearance, Edwina stood there and stared at her mother. Her arms came up to return the welcoming embrace.

Her mother looked Edwina full in the face and rushed to Olivia, being helped out of the lead wagon by Case. She gave Olivia the loving embrace, the mother's kiss, and the words of welcome. Olivia and the girls were petted and hugged, cried over, and hugged again, by both Edwina's mother and her aunt Jean.

Beyond hurt, numb to all feeling, and not even wondering how her mother had gotten to Oregon, Edwina just stood there. She watched until Olivia pulled away from their mother. Her words were loud enough to carry to Edwina. "Where is Ambrose?"

"He's in there," her mother answered, gesturing toward the saloon.

"He will be expecting me to come to him."

"Wait! He's very upset about what happened out there and he needs a little more—"

Olivia gave her mother a quick kiss on the cheek. "He's my husband, Mother. I have to go to him. It is a wife's duty."

Dark skirts flaring, she whirled abruptly, and walked down the boardwalk toward Edwina, stopping just before she reached her to step down into the street. She started across, holding up her skirts to keep them from the litter of horse manure.

The wind was colder. The entire town was an ugly gray. Almost overwhelmed by a foreboding so great it almost sickened her, Edwina shivered. Tal was striding down the boardwalk toward her, but there was no time to do more than give him a final look.

Taking a deep breath, she turned her back to him.

Chapter Twenty

If Tal had had a choice, he wouldn't be anywhere near Ambrose Raiter, his whiskey, his guns, or his town. But here he was back where he started and no way to remake the past or alter the future.

Nothing much had changed, he thought wryly. Except now he was half-blind besides being flat broke, in love with a woman he couldn't have, and still cold to the marrow of his bones. No matter what he wanted, this part of his journey was over. He reined in the mules, wrapped the lines around the brake handle, and stared straight ahead.

The hard wooden seat hurt his rear, his feet felt like two chunks of ice, and his hands weren't a hell of a lot better. He didn't try to reduce his discomfort by moving around to warm up his cold extremities. Tal just sat there, thinking about the way things were.

It wasn't like he didn't know what he ought to do—what he had to do. That was clear as a summer sky, but that damned sure didn't mean he had to like it. Oh, he'd sell the gelding all right, get enough money to catch the first stage south, and . . .

The wagon creaked as he shifted on the seat. It sounded too much like the cracking of dreams. Pulling the grimy slicker a little tighter around his slumped shoulders, Tal glared at nothing in particular. He scratched at his dirty beard with a gloved finger and thought wistfully of a bath and a trip to the barbershop. He wasn't a vain man, but it would be nice if Edwina could see him just once . . .

He had to catch the next stage. It was the only decent thing to do.

A nail-bitten, grubby hand grabbed at his arm and gave it a little shake. "You be Jones, ain'tcha?" The voice wasn't familiar and he couldn't see well enough to recognize any of the man's features. Not wanting to let on how blind he really was, Tal turned his head, looked straight at the blob, and nodded.

"The boss said to tell you, you done good," the man said, snickering as his breath came near to polluting the frigid air with the sour smell of stale whiskey, onions, and rotting teeth.

Tal didn't have to ask who the boss was—it had to be Raiter. Sure the boss' messenger had more to say, Tal waited without speaking.

"Said to give ya this," the man said, holding something out.

Catching the yellowish glint of gold, Tal extended his hand, palm up.

"Two double eagles. That's right, ain't it?"

"For what?"

"That be between you and the boss."

The man snickered and was gone. Tal was tempted to throw Raiter's money in the dirt, but he didn't. He gripped it tightly while he tried to think.

He heard Edwina's wagon pull into town and crawl to a stop behind the others. He stuffed the gold coins into his vest pocket and climbed down from the wagon, stepping onto the boardwalk. He knew just how helpless he was to change anything that was going to happen.

"Jones, I gotta to talk to you."

"What—?"

188

"Shhhh! It's Miz Raiter's mother and her aunt. They walked right past the kid."

Before Tal could answer, Larson gripped his arm and warned, "They're coming."

Tal didn't have to ask *who*, he could hear them. Becca, Meg, and their mother were being greeted by the grandmother and the aunt. It sounded like a grand family reunion—one that didn't include Edwina.

He jerked free, left Larson standing on the boardwalk, and headed toward Edwina's wagon, but he knew before he got there that he was too late. She had already marched into the street, following her sister. He would have stepped into the street right behind her, but Crocker, sipping whiskey from his canteen, jumped in front of him and stopped him in his tracks.

"Get out of my way."

Case caught up to them. "What are you jawing about, Crock?"

He snickered and pointed at Case. "Hell, Case, you ain't so all-fired smart. Tal here, he knew all along, I reckon."

"Dammit, Crock, spit out what's eating you or get the hell out of the way."

Snickering again, Crocker continued, "Ed Parker, the kid, is Lobo Chance. And, ole Tal here could likely tell you first-hand that Lobo Chance ain't no boy."

Doubling up his fist, Tal caught Crocker on the point of the chin and sat him on his butt. "You say one more word about Edwina," Tal threatened quietly, "and I'll be real happy to put a bullet in your gut."

"Mama, noooooooooooo!" Becca's cry was a howl of despair. "Auntie Jean, stop her."

There was a commotion on the walk, but Edwina didn't

look back. Whatever it was could take care of itself.

Edwina's mother and aunt were making soothing sounds.

Edwina followed her sister across the street. Her mouth set, she pushed open one of the swinging doors and stepped into smoky interior of Raiter's saloon. She halted just inside the batwing and tried to stifle the cough caused by inhaling whiskey fumes and cigar smoke. The warmth was a welcomed change, even if her icy hands started to tingle and her nose itched. Edwina stood and watched in silence as her sister walked slowly across the room to her husband.

Arrogant, handsome in a florid, overblown way, Ambrose didn't move to greet his wife, except to lift a glass to his mouth and swallow a healthy slug of whiskey. Pink-jowled, clean-shaven, he waited. His dark hair glistening with Macassar oil, his full lips twisted in a sneer, he leaned against the long wooden bar and watched his wife with glittering eyes.

It took forever for Olivia cross the space between them. There was more than time enough for the burly barkeep to move down to one end of the bar and pretend he was doing his job and not watching every move his boss made. More than enough time for the two men drinking at the bar to pick up their bottle and glasses and move to one of the tables. More than enough time for Raiter to take another long drink of whiskey and set the glass down, clicking it against the surface of the long bar.

Outside the wind moaned and whistled. Footsteps echoed, sounding hollow and faraway as booted feet trod on the boardwalk. Women's voices climbed shrill, barely penetrating the interior of the saloon. Men's voices, deeper and heavier, were clearer, but still only rumbles of sound.

Inside, only Olivia's feet whispering across the layer of sand on the floor and Ambrose's harsh breathing disturbed the gloom until Ambrose Raiter snarled, "You whoring slut, it's about time you drug your sorry ass into town."

"I'm so sorry, Ambrose. I—I had the girls to think of . . ." Olivia said, her voice a begging whisper. Regardless of how weak she seemed, she kept on walking until she was directly in front of her husband. She stood there, hands clasped before her bosom, head bowed, and waited for the punishment he was going to mete out for her transgressions.

He straightened up and glared at Livy. "You mealy-mouthed whore, if you didn't have the guts to do the right thing, I ought to do it for you, kill you for shaming me like this. I'll never be able to run for public office after this."

For just a moment, Edwina thought that was what he was going to do. As he reached toward the revolver strapped around his waist, her fingers unbuttoned her coat and shoved it out of the way, giving her easy access to the holstered Colt. She took two steps forward, knowing she was fully visible to her brother-in-law, if he cared to look. He didn't seem to be so inclined. Knowing he was sly, besides being a liar and a bully, Edwina didn't trust outward appearances.

"Ambrose, I—I—I pray for your forgiveness. I know—"

"Know what?" he asked. "Know that tame preacher of your ma's would be the first to tell you that any decent, God-fearing woman would choose death before dishonor? Woman, by spreading your legs for another man, you have sinned against your husband and your church. Is that any way for a Christian woman like you, a wife and a mother, to act?"

Edwina knew he was baiting Livy, but Livy seemed to be accepting every ugly, degrading word that came from his mouth. She said meekly, "Yes, Ambrose, and I know what the preacher would say, and I—I have begged the Lord for forgiveness for my sins. If you can't afford me the same forgiveness, I would ask that you, as is your right before man and God, put me aside as your wife and—"

He straightened, drew back his hand, and slapped her hard enough to knock her dusty bonnet askew. "Put you aside, hell."

"Please, Ambrose, I beg you, think on it. Edwina has money. She would pay for the divorce and—"

He laughed, but there was no mirth in it, only cold fury. "No, Olivia. I figure, since you like bedding other men so much, I'm gonna put you to work upstairs and get some use out of you. You'll like that, won't you?"

"No, Ambrose, I'm your wife. The mother of your daughters." Livy's voice rose, holding a multitude of unshed tears. "You can't do this. What will . . ."

Time seemed to stop entirely. Everything took on a sheen of light. Edwina saw the saloon with startling clarity: the tobacco-stained spittoons, the brass rail on the bar, the large painting of the nude behind the bar, the shiny tin reflectors behind the lamps set on shelves behind the bar and hanging from brackets on the walls, the pot bellied stoves at either end of the room, and the two tired-looking women on the stairs to the upper floor of the saloon.

Livy. Weary. Clothes wrinkled and dirty. Terror in every line of her thin body.

Ambrose. His pig eyes glittering with hate. His mouth twisted.

And Edwina knew someone in the saloon was going to die.

"Our girls," Olivia cried. "You can't do this to—"

Laughing again, acting as if the whole pitiful scene was a comedy staged just for his benefit. He slapped her again, and the sound of his palm hitting her cheek cracked like a rifle shot.

Olivia staggered, almost went down, righted herself, and attacked. Screaming incoherently, she leaped at him and clawed his face with taloned hands. Scratching a long furrow in his right cheek, she brought first blood. He fought her off by shoving one of his large hands against her face. She caught his little finger between her teeth and bit down hard.

His face red and contorted, Ambrose Raiter screamed. The agony didn't put a halt to his rage, or stop him from drawing back his other hand. Almost before Edwina could gasp in a breath, Ambrose clenched his large hand into a fist and slammed it into his wife's belly hard enough to lift her off her feet and throw her away from him.

Her mouth still dark with his blood, Olivia landed on her side. Stunned by the blow, she lay there without moving. The moment stretched long enough for Edwina to narrow her eyes, focus on Ambrose, flex her gun hand, and take several steps forward.

Moaning, Oliva curled into a ball. "Help me," she said, the words coming out in a whimper. "Please, someone help me."

Her voice one with the mourning wind, Edwina could hear her mother crying outside the door and begging Ambrose to stop.

"Help me."

Edwina didn't look away from her brother-in-law. She knew the other men in the saloon were shame-faced, but unwilling to interfere between a man and his wife.

Ambrose drew back a booted foot.

"That's enough," Edwina said, taking another step toward him.

Looking at her, really seeing her for the first time, he laughed uproariously before he completed the kick, the toe of his boot catching Olivia on the hip.

Moaning, she twisted away from her husband, pushed at the gritty floor with both hands, raised herself to her knees, and began scuttling back. But not until she looked at Edwina, her voice colored with pain and despair. "Mr. Chance, please. I beg you, help me."

Creaking on its hinges, the saloon door swung open behind her, but Edwina didn't look around. Her hand hovering over her gun butt, she narrowed her eyes, and said again, "That's enough, Raiter."

His laughter turned harsh. "Do your damnedest, Mr. Chance," he said mockingly. "I'm not afraid of any woman alive. If you're planning on drawing on me, then I'd be real pleased to see a vinegar-tongued spinster like you dead and buried."

Raiter knew who she was, but Edwina didn't have time to worry the how of that. She watched his eyes and knew when he went for his gun. The world narrowed until it held only the two of them—and their revolvers. She saw him jerk his six-shooter from the holster before her hand closed on the grip of her Colt.

It was in her hand, the muzzle coming up to point at his chest, when she heard the explosion.

Felt the lead nip her ear.

Squeezed off her shot.

Felt the revolver buck in her hand.

Saw fire blaze from the barrel of the Colt.

Watched as red blossomed, spread on the front of his white shirt, ran between the fingers of the hand that dropped its gun and came up to clutch at his chest as he crumpled sideways and went down hard.

Men shouted.

She ignored them. Unable to move, Edwina stood there for a long moment. When her senses returned in a rush, she walked over and looked down at Ambrose Raiter. She knew she ought to feel sorry, but she didn't. She was glad he was dead. Despite her feelings, her hand was shaking violently when she tried to holster the Colt. Bitter gall was rising in her throat.

She was sick to her very soul, but her voice was steady when she said the first thing that came to mind, "How did he know that Lobo Chance was a woman?"

"The whole town knows, Miss Parkhurst, ma'am," the barkeep said, tugging at his forelock. "That publisher of yours sent a telegram a week ago, telling everybody who Lobo Chance was. It came as a right big surprise to—" he jerked his head toward Raiter's body— "and to your ma."

He stood there, looking at her for a moment. "Of course, the boss didn't know you was a gunfighter for true, did he, ma'am?"

"No, I don't suppose . . ."

Olivia tugged at Edwina's arm and pulled her around so that they were standing face to face. "Oh, Edwina, I—I . . ." Olivia gasped between sobs, "You shouldn't have . . . I didn't mean for you to kill him. He was . . ."

Unable to continue, she reached out and touched Edwina's ear. "You're bleeding." Olivia looked at the blood on her hand, her face pale beneath its tears, and fainted. One of the men clustered around Raiter caught her as she fell and laid her on the floor beside her dead husband.

The barkeep said, "Miz Raiter's ma's outside, somebody get her."

Mrs. Parkhurst hadn't waited to be called. Leaving Jean outside with the weeping girls, she ran to her fallen daughter, knelt on the filthy floor, and held a vial of smelling salts beneath Olivia's nose. Murmuring endearments, she soothed her elder daughter and gave soft-voiced orders for Olivia to be transported, by willing male arms to the hotel. Her mother fussed and worried, but never once, by even so much as a glance, did she acknowledge Edwina's existence.

Physically ill, Edwina turned abruptly and headed for the door.

Hands grabbed at her. A harsh voice shouted, "Stop Chance, he's—she's getting away."

Chapter Twenty-One

The gunshot, followed quickly by another, came from Raiter's saloon, and they frightened Tal into a cold sweat. Edwina was in there facing Raiter alone without Tal to back her up.

His knuckles still smarting from the blow he'd delivered, he forgot Crocker and Case. Talmadge Jones even forgot that he was blind. Edwina was in trouble and he had to reach her. Leaping from the boardwalk, he hit the street running and was nearly across when he stumbled over a pile of horse dung.

Case Larson caught him by the arm, dragged him back to his feet, and released his grip as they reached the other side. "Come on," Case growled. "Whatever happens, I'm with you."

Someone was crying softly. He couldn't see her, but he knew it wasn't Edwina, and she was the only woman in his life who mattered.

Evidently Case had other concerns. He stopped long enough to ask, "Becca? What—"

"Grandma just went in that place. I heard a man say Lobo Chance killed my father. Something's wrong with Mama now. Maybe she's dead, too."

Strangers' voices added new information to Tal's meager store. Whatever had happened in Raiter's, it was causing a stir in the growing crowd and that couldn't be good. He might not be able to see what was going on, but Tal could hear, and his fear for Edwina's safety increased.

"Damned if Lobo Chance didn't draw and shoot Raiter before he even went for his gun."

"The boss never stood a chance."

"Hell, I don't care if Lobo Chance is a female. She ain't getting away with shooting down Raiter's wife!"

"Don't be a fool! Raiter's wife ain't dead!"

"I saw her fall. Blood all over her. I say, get a rope and—"

The wind was coming out of the north, carrying a full load of ice pellets and sleet stung the back of Tal's neck. The wind tried to lift the hat from his head. As cold as it was, he was sweating hard and praying. He had almost reached the door when he saw Raiter's hangers-on draw back and move away from the tall, thin figure that stalked out of the saloon.

For just a second, what was left of his vision blurred. "Edwina," he said, barely breathing her name as he reached for her and tried to look at her face.

"Mama? Is Mama dead? Did you kill her, too?" Becca's cry was sharper than the wind.

"Hush, child," a woman said, sounding irritated. "I told you your mother swooned. There's nothing wrong with her. Stop this unseemly display right now."

Case was standing at Tal's shoulder. He said, "The kid's been shot. Her ear's bleeding, Jones. Looks like just a nick. Get her away from here and I'll—"

"Nobody's taking Chance anywhere until we—"

Releasing Edwina, Tal turned and pushed the slicker away from his holstered gun. "Just who plans on stopping me?"

Nobody answered him directly, but one of the men said, "It's Jones. The gunfighter."

Another man said, "Hell, it's too damned cold to stand around arguing. Get that marshal Raiter hired last week. Let him settle it when he sobers up."

"Yeah, well, he'd better do it damned soon. I'm needing a drink and Raiter's ain't serving right now."

"If the marshal wants to talk to Miss Parkhurst," Tal said, "she'll be waiting at the hotel after she's seen the doctor."

He waited a moment longer. "Any objections?"

"Naw, Jones," Case declared. "I'll stay here."

Turning back to Edwina, Tal put his arm around her shoulders and ordered, "Come on."

They were across the street and nearing the hotel before she started to shake. Tal knew the feeling. He also knew she didn't need to be where people could stare at her, but it was too cold to linger outside.

"Tal," she whispered through chattering teeth, "I can't go in there yet. I'm going to be sick—"

"Okay, just hang on. I'll get you out of here."

They were past the entrance to the hotel, around the corner, and heading down toward the Summer River, before she swallowed hard. "Raiter's dead. I killed him."

"Yes," he said gruffly.

"I didn't think it would be . . . He shot first, but when I shot . . . I saw the bullet hit and the blood. He was kicking Olivia. I had to shoot him, but I didn't know . . . Oh, Tal, he was an evil man, but killing him hurts."

"Yes," he said again. "I know." He did know. He knew there wasn't a thing he could do to make it any easier for her. She had killed a man, and she would have to live with it the rest of her life.

She would have to pay a hard price for that killing every day of her life—Tal knew about that, too. How it set you apart and how law-abiding folks never, never forgot. *Or forgave.*

"Tal, I'm—I'm . . ." She gulped, swallowed, gulped again as he got her into the shelter of a clump of winter-bare willows before she went to her knees and started heaving. Tal held her head while she vomited, washed her face with water from the stream, and murmured meaningless words of encouragement.

And then, not worrying that the leaves were a frozen mass, or that the snow was coming down hard, he scraped a few branches out of a small washout under a bank of earth. Then he sat down, pulled her onto his lap, wrapped his slicker around them both, and held her against his heart. He waited without words until she started to cry.

She cried for a long time. He couldn't really see it, but he knew the snow was drifting ahead of the wind and night was coming. It was past time he took her back to her family. He would do that soon. For now, he just held her, knowing it was probably the last time he would ever touch her.

Her sobs had faded to an occasional hiccup, but she was still warm against him when Case Larson came to the edge of the willow thicket and called, "You in there, Jones?"

Edwina surprised him. She snuggled closer before she answered, her voice giving away nothing of her feelings, "Yes, Mr. Larson, we both are."

Case pushed through the clattering branches and stood over them. He said, "Kid, I mean, Miss Parkhurst, your ma's—

"Hell's bells, you know how Jake is about that sister of yours and she's having the vapors. That damned—excuse me, kid—the marshal was there and he's not listening to much in the way of reason.

"Kid, your ma is trying to get moved out of the hotel and into Raiter's house. She said they'd be a heap more comfortable in a house. So Jake reckoned you'd best come and see what you can do about fixing up this mess you made for Miz Raiter and the rest of your family."

Anger rising within him, Tal stiffened. Edwina laid her hand on his lips and whispered, "No, Tal, don't. Mr. Larson's right. One way or another, I do have to go back and fix the mess I've made of my life. Of all our lives."

Taking in a deep breath and letting it out in a gusty sigh, Case spoke to Edwina. "According to Jake, your ma's of the opinion that you're hiding out, afraid to tell her that you've been playing the fool with Jones here, whilst your sister was being dishonored."

Edwina sat up and pulled away from Tal's sheltering arms. Her voice was cold when she replied, "Mr. Larson, you know as well as I that Talmadge Jones is a man of honor and—"

"This ain't none of my saying, kid. Your ma knows who he is, and what he is—a lot of folks have seen to that. The truth is, you spent a lot of nights alone in his company and, the way she sees it, it just ain't fitting for a lady." Case stopped abruptly, swore loudly, and fought his way out of the thicket.

Tal knew they had to go back and say their final farewells. "I'll walk you to the hotel and have a little talk with the marshal," he said as she scrambled to her feet.

They went side by side through the blowing snow. His arm was around her, but they were both silent.

He was reaching to push the lobby door open when she looked up at him. "I love you, Tal. No matter what happens now, I always will, but I can't desert them."

Her quiet words hurt more than the silence. It was the hurt that choked his voice when he said, "I know, how I know."

Aunt Jean, a short woman, her graying hair braided tight and wound around her head like a crown, seemed smaller and more fearful than Edwina remembered. Edwina wanted to go to her and offer a small measure of comfort. Jean didn't want Edwina's embrace anyway. Her gaze barely touched her niece and skittered away before their eyes met. She wouldn't look at Edwina, but she glowered at Tal.

Looking at the sour disapproving expression on her aunt's usually pleasant face, she said, "Aunt Jean," expecting to be castigated and reprimanded, not only for her unseemly acts but also for her attire.

Her expression going from disapproval to a curious mixture of fear and disapproval, Jean's voice sounded strained and unfamiliar, "Your mother asked me to wait for you here, Edwina, and—and . . ."

In great distress, Jean's gloved fingers twisted together and in the dimly lit, unfinished lobby of the hotel, Edwina could see the red rising to mottle her aunt's face. Thinking Jean was near a swoon, Edwina stepped away from Tal and moved toward her.

Jean's hands flew apart, palms extended at arms' length in front of her black-clad figure. For an instant, Edwina didn't know what was wrong. Thinking her aunt was ill, she took another step toward her and Jean shrank away. Then Edwina knew.

She wasn't just the old maid niece anymore, she was Edwina Parkhurst, gun-fighter, cold-blooded killer, a sinner to be feared and shunned.

"Your sister insisted that Martha—" Jean pointed toward the crude stair that led to the upper floor of the hotel. "She's tending the man who was shot."

Her hands fluttered again before coming together at her waist, clutching each other, and clinging tightly as her voice took on a querulous tone. "This town and Ambrose's house is bad enough. I don't know what Olivia expects us to do without Martha. Who is going to cook and—"

It wasn't a complaint Edwina wanted to hear. She interrupted, "Am I to stay here?"

Shaking her head, Jean fairly bustled around. She pulled a

heavy cloak around her with air of righteous determination, and walked toward the door.

"There are many chores to be done and no one to . . . Your mother needs you, Edwina, but he can stay here," she said, not looking in Tal's direction, disapproval coloring every word. "Mr. Larson—Mr. Jake, not his brother—wants to see him as soon as possible and Mr. Milch has kindly volunteered to escort us to Ambrose's house."

She couldn't follow her aunt out of the hotel and leave Tal in the cold, empty lobby with its brass spittoons and odors of unwashed bodies.

"Oh, Tal, I—I can't . . ." New tears welling in her eyes, clogging her throat, she reached out blindly and touched his bearded face with trembling fingers.

"Edwina Parkhurst!" Jean's shocked exclamation cut between them, brought Edwina to what was left of her senses. Knowing there was nothing more to be said, she stood there for just a moment and let her hand linger on the coarseness of his whiskers. She whispered, "Good-bye."

The first two fingers of his right hand, still icy from the storm, touched his lips first and then hers, transferring a final, gentle kiss before she walked out the door. She didn't look back.

The storm hit her full in the face, but Edwina didn't bow her head before its fury. She welcomed it and the over-whelming weariness that numbed her mind and soul when, at last, they reached Ambrose Raiter's small house and she readied herself to face her family.

Jean pushed the door open and entered, but Milch caught Edwina by the arm just as she stepped up on the uneven stone that served as a stoop. "Kid," he said, leaning in close so she could hear him above the howl of the freezing wind, "give them a little time."

Surprised and touched by his words, she managed to say, "Thank you," but nothing more before he touched his hand to his hat, turned, and plunged back into the snowstorm. Shivering with cold, she stood there and watched the whirling, blowing flakes. Sighing, she pushed the rough door open and stepped into what was now her sister's house— thanks to Edwina's bullet.

The parlor, with its red carpet, three red-and-gold plush settees, rose-bedecked wallpaper, and potbellied heater, was better furnished and more finished-looking than Edwina expected. It was still tawdry, ugly with its excess of mirrors, vases, feathers, hassocks, and too much red.

Her family was there, and not one of them looked at her as she stepped into the room and closed the heavy door behind her. Waiting for someone to say something, she watched them. Maybe one of them would smile at her and say, "Hello, Edwina, we were worried sick about you. Thank the Good Lord you're safe."

Hair long and loose, freshly washed and drying in the warmth, Olivia and her daughters were dressed in clean but wrinkled flannel wrappers, all bought just prior to leaving for the West with Edwina's sinful earnings. Their clean faces still bore evidence of the horrors they had undergone, but it was, nonetheless, a peaceful scene, one Edwina had seen many times in the past.

Running combs through their long tresses, the three were sitting on hassocks around the stove. There was no sign that they had been weeping for Ambrose. Aunt Jean had removed her cloak and was standing between the two girls, with her back to Edwina, silently warming herself.

Sipping tea from a delicate china cup, Edwina's mother sat on the edge of one of the settees. Her face was thin, bloodless, and crumpled-looking. Her eyes were sunken, surrounded by heavy purple shadows, and her hands were trembling so badly she was having trouble holding the cup.

Love for them almost overwhelmed Edwina. She wanted to beg for forgiveness, but it was too late for that. She took a step forward into the pale light that came from four lamps. Hesitating, she cleared her throat.

Setting the cup back into its saucer, her mother's soft voice held censure. "Olivia and the girls have bathed. It's probably quite cold by now, but it was saved for you. You'll find suitable garments laid out in the kitchen. When you are decent, we will talk."

She spoke to Edwina, but didn't look at her after the first quick furtive glance that caused her mouth to grimace with distaste.

Edwina wasn't hurt by her mother's attitude. Leaving Tal, knowing they were truly parted, had been all the hurt her heart could absorb. She felt distanced, as if her family were nearly strangers, people she had known and loved in another life. The thought shook her badly. Looking at the women and children whose welfare had once been her whole reason for being, she tried to smile at them, but wasn't terribly successful.

She did manage to croak out, "Yes, Mother," before she walked wearily across the room and through the curtained door in the rear, searching for the slipper tub and its soap-scummed water. It was sitting in front of the stove. One lamp did little to chase away the shadows, but it gave enough light for her to see. An empty copper wash boiler was on the wooden floor. A teakettle sat on the back of the stove, but it would do little to warm her bath with the fire burned down to ash.

Thinking of the baths she had taken in the hot spring back in the canyon, Edwina stood looking down at the pile of wrinkled garments that had been laid out for her to wear. As if she was uncertain as to their exact nature, she picked up the petticoats, the skirt, the drawers, the corset cover, and examined them. She looked longest at the corset that was so prominently displayed, an unspoken reproof of her current and definitely unseemly attire. She smiled as she picked it up, walked over to the stove, lifted a lid, and used the instrument of female torture to kindle a new fire. One she would use to heat clean bathwater for herself.

Chapter Twenty-Two

While the boiler full of water, pumped from the hand pump she had found in the enclosed porch behind the kitchen, heated for her bath, Edwina prowled through the platters, pots, and pans on the back of the stove, in the warming oven, and on the round oak table. It wasn't a very successful foraging attempt, but she managed to treat her grumbling stomach to two cold biscuits, several bites of cold ham, and a spoonful of a congealed something that might have once been gravy.

It didn't rest easy in her empty stomach. It did give her enough energy to dump the slimy water in the slipper tub, refill it, peel off her filthy garments, climb into the hot water, and soap off layer after layer of trail grime and campfire grease.

She was dawdling and she knew it. She wasn't yet ready to face her mother and be damned as a sinner. Edwina's mouth twisted into a wry smile.

Had she been wrong to take care of all of them over the years? Had her care turned them into selfish, ignorant women? It wasn't something she could worry about at the moment, so she tucked the thought away for future appraisal.

Her crown of unevenly hacked-off hair curling damply around her head, cold air creeping under her skirts to chill her lower limbs and stockinged feet, she tossed the filthy garments she had removed into the wash boiler. She filled it again and set long johns, shirt, and britches to soak until she could give them a good scrubbing with lye soap. She picked up the coat the muleskinner had given her and folded it carefully. She held it against her cheek, breathing in the smells of mule, sweat, and a love that came too late. She took the coat out to the enclosed porch and hid it behind some wooden crates, so no one would throw it away.

After she emptied her bathwater and tidied the clutter, she knew she had done everything possible to delay her return to the living room. She might be more suitably dressed, at least from her mother's point of view, but Edwina doubted that her family would ever again consider her decent. Redemption, at least in her family's eyes, wasn't possible for a fallen woman.

Taking a deep breath, she wiped the palms of her hands down the billowing sides of the blue serge skirt she wore. It belonged to Olivia and was too big around the waist, too short at the bottom and not as warm as the britches she'd been wearing. She tugged impatiently at the lace-trimmed, ribbon-banded bodice, picked up the Colt, neatly wrapped in the gun belt, and walked toward the curtain-hung doorway. She was pushing the length of heavy velvet aside when her aunt's words of judgment stopped her.

"And you might be inclined to Christian charity, but I'm telling you that I saw him with my own two eyes. It was easy to see the man's a cold-blooded killer, evil as they come, a sinner bound straight for hell." She paused for an instant and then went on. "The nerve of him. A heathen with no regard for anyone or anything."

"Mr. Jones saved my life, Aunt Jean. Saved the girls."

Edwina's mother was blunt. "He is a murderer. Edwina is ruined. There's no doubt of that, but—oh, dear, I can't even look at her. All the years of lies and sin, and now this. She is my daughter, but I feel so helpless. I don't know my own child, but I do know she isn't the same person that we loved and respected."

Jean was pacing. Edwina could hear the slide of her slippers across the nap of the carpet and the swish of her skirts as she turned. "Isn't it enough that she has shamed us before man and God? Do we have to allow her to continue this alliance?"

"I will speak to her, Auntie," Olivia said, sounding as tired as Edwina felt. "I'll try to make her understand why Mr. Jones is—"

Pushing the curtain aside, Edwina took a deep breath and stepped into the parlor. A muscle twitched in her jaw, but her voice was level and her tone mild when she said, "I know what Mr. Jones is, Livy, a man of integrity. I can assure you that you have nothing to worry about as far as he is concerned. His intentions toward me are honorable, but they do not include marriage. Nor would I accept such an offer if it was intended only to save my reputation. Mr. Jones and I have parted, so, as soon you have buried your husband, settled your affairs here, and can dispose of Ambrose's property, I will wire the bank for a letter of credit. When it arrives, we can take the next stage to Winnemucca and return home."

One of the lamps was gone, as were the two girls, but there was still light enough to see the quick look her mother and aunt exchanged. Her mother's face flushed before she said, pushing the words out quickly, but speaking with determination underlying every word, "Edwina, we are not going back to—we can't."

"Can't? Why?" Edwina rubbed at her temples hoping to ward off the headache that was beginning to throb there.

"There's nothing to go back to," Jean said.

"Our home? All—"

"Gone," her mother said weakly. "All gone."

"How? Fire? Mother, what are you . . ." Her voice rising, echoing Edwina's feelings of disbelief, Olivia asked the same startled questions that were rampaging through Edwina's mind.

"No, dear, not fire. It was just that . . ." Their mother reached out, took Olivia's hand, and looked only at her elder daughter when she made her rather halting explanation. "You see, after you left that publisher of Edwina's came, and he said . . . He told us about—about Edwina's writing. We were so shocked that we—we talked to the reverend and asked him for guidance, and he . . ."

Remembering every hour she had spent in researching and writing the little books, every rejection she had gotten along the way, every lie that she had felt forced to tell, Edwina took a deep breath, squeezed her hands into fists, and clamped her teeth together. It wasn't enough.

Anger surged through her. "And that damned idiot who calls himself a man of God did what, Mother? Besides damning me to the fires of hell, what did he talk you into doing with *my* house?"

"It wasn't your house," Jean quavered, giving the Colt Edwina still held a quick, fearful glance. "You put your mother's name on the deed. It was paid for with sin."

Stark disbelief replaced Edwina's anger, and in turn, gave way to comprehension. That and an incredible, over-whelming weariness making her voice mild, she stated, "You gave my house to the preacher." It wasn't a question, it was a statement of fact.

"To the church," her mother corrected. "We asked the reverend and he agreed that was the only way he knew that would erase some of the shame you brought upon the family."

"What about the furnishings?" Olivia asked quietly. "Did you—"

"Yes, dear, we donated everything," Mrs. Parkhurst answered, her voice dropping to a whisper, one that could barely be heard over the crackling of the fire in the heater and the wail of the storm outside.

Swallowing hard, Edwina walked over to the small window at the far end of the parlor, pulled aside the heavy drapery and leaned her forehead against the icy pane. Chaotic thoughts tore at her. What was she going to do? No house. No furnishings. And very probably no money left in the bank either—except in the one account. The one that was in her name alone. They couldn't have touched that, could they?

Behind her, she heard Olivia ask, "Everything? You gave the church everything we owned?"

Her mother was crying—Edwina didn't have to turn away from the window to know that. Her mother always wept when things were unpleasant.

"Yes, dear, everything except our clothes and a few personal items."

"And what we found in that writing place in the attic." Jean's whisper dropped even lower. "We burned that."

She might as well have called Edwina's writing desk a den of iniquity, her tone implied it was exactly that. Edwina grieved for all that was lost. "How and where did you expect to live, Mother?"

"Ambrose is—was Olivia's husband. The reverend said the Lord would provide. He was sure Ambrose had learned his lesson and would do his Christian duty. We came here because it is his duty to provide for us."

"Was he planning on making you and Aunt Jean calico queens, too? Send you upstairs over the saloon? Make you work for your keep like he threatened Olivia?" Born of frustration, anger, and grief, the words were out before Edwina could call them back. She dropped the window covering, cradled Tal's six-gun, and turn to look at the three women who were huddled around the heater.

"Please," Olivia whispered. "They don't know. I didn't tell them what—what Ambrose . . . what he said."

"Or that you begged me to shoot him? You let them think I killed the bastard because I hated him?"

"Yes. No, I . . . Oh, Edwina, I'm sorry."

"Sorry doesn't change a damned thing, Olivia. Not one damned thing," Edwina snapped. "Tell them the truth, every ugly bit of it, before they decide to give your wagon loads of rotgut whiskey, your cases of rifles, your saloon, and your whorehouse to the church, too."

"Ohhhhh," Mrs. Parkhurst moaned, slumping against the back of the settee.

"Shame on you. Talking like a—" Jean cried.

Edwina ignored her mother and aunt and looked at Olivia. "Well?"

Taking a deep breath, Olivia nodded. She told the two older women the full truth of what had happened in the saloon. Why Edwina had shot Ambrose, that he had threatened to shoot her or use her in the rooms above the stairs.

Jean got to her feet, and said, "I don't believe a word of it. No Christian man would treat his wife that way. Olivia, he was just upset about what happened to you. You must have misunderstood."

"No, Auntie," Edwina said quietly, "she didn't misunderstand."

Mrs. Parkhurst stood also, and moving slowly, as if she had aged dreadfully in the past few minutes, she touched Jean's arm before she picked up one of the lamps. "Come,"

They walked to a doorway hidden behind one of the settees and disappeared. Edwina's heart ached to see how feeble they were.

She stood where she was after the older women were gone, listening to the wind howling and wishing that she were with Tal. Edwina sighed.

Lifting her head at the small sound, Olivia spoke softly. "Edwina, I pretended not to know you back there at that horrible place, because I was so ashamed."

"It's over. Don't worry about it. I imagine I'll shame you again before—"

Olivia cried, "I wasn't ashamed of you. I was . . . Edwina, I . . . That man violated me, but I didn't want to do the right thing. I know I should have tried to kill myself, but I didn't want to die. The girls needed me. I couldn't face you, couldn't stand to see the condemnation in your eyes. God help me, I couldn't. Not after I had accused you of a lesser sin."

Edwina walked across the floor and knelt in front of her sister. She touched her wet cheeks with gentle fingers. "Livy, it wasn't like that at all. I would never condemn you for what someone else did to you—especially when it was all Ambrose's fault to begin with. I thought you denied knowing me because you were ashamed of me."

Olivia wasn't finished. "Edwina, I love you, and I know how much you have done for me over the years. And, may God forgive me for being an ungrateful, selfish fool. This experience could have destroyed me, but I found I could survive for my girls. I'm just beginning to realize how hard you must have worked and how much you gave up for us." She took a quick breath. "Sister, what Mama let the preacher talk her into was wrong, I know it now, but I can't change it. This house isn't very big, and you're going to have to sleep on a pallet until we can get another bed. But as long as I have a home, it is yours as much as it is mine. Yours, and Mama's, and Aunt Jean's. I owe you so much more than I can ever—" Overcome, Olivia couldn't go on. She sat on the hassock, her lower lip quivering.

Edwina patted her knee, got to her feet. "Thank you for the offer. I might even have to take you up on it, but I think we're too tired to worry about this anymore tonight. Tomorrow isn't going to be easy." She leaned over and kissed her older sister's forehead. "You go on. I'll tend the fires and the lamps and make sure the doors are latched."

Olivia grabbed Edwina's skirt and held her in place. "Please, Edwina," she begged, "don't take this wrong. I love you and don't want you to . . . Please, don't make the same mistake I did."

The plea didn't make sense. "What do you mean, the same mistake you did?"

"Edwina, I know you think you care for Mr. Jones, but I thought that about Ambrose. I didn't realize what kind of man he was until it was too late. You don't have to go through that, Edwina. You know what Mr. Jones is. You know that he isn't good enough for you or any decent woman. He's a gunfighter, a killer. He's not fit for proper society. He's an outcast."

"Really? Has it occurred to you that I killed your husband this afternoon, Olivia? That I shot him with this very Colt after he drew on me? He shot first, but, no matter what you think, it was a gunfight." There was only the smallest of quavers in Edwina's voice when she looked at her sister and asked, "What does that make me?"

Tal went to the bathhouse and the barbershop, came out clean, shorn, and smelling of bay rum, but he didn't go to the burying. He intended to go, after he sold the gelding to the livery stable owner and checked to see when the stage was coming in again, but his plans were changed by Case Larson.

The storm had blown itself out sometime during the night, leaving behind small drifts of ice pellets and rippled sand. The air was sharp, carrying wood smoke and sage in its teeth. The sun cast a bright light but held no warmth at all.

Tal shivered as he stepped out of the hotel lobby. His clothes were at the laundry, but Edwina's box of writing was tucked safe under his left arm. After the words had been said over Raiter's remains, Tal was going to take the writing to Edwina. He would tell her good-bye, if he could, and hike to the hotel to wait for the morning stage.

"Jones?" Case Larson stepped onto the walk in front of him. "I need to talk to you."

Tal's sight had improved considerably. Images were still blurred, but Tal could almost make out Case's features.

"About what?" Tal asked.

"You didn't go see Jake last night."

"So?"

Case shuffled his feet and cleared his throat. "Jake ain't exactly himself since he met Miz Raiter."

Tal wanted to grin at the man's discomfort, but he didn't. "What does he want now?"

"Well, Jake had a little talk with the marshal. Dammit, Jones, the idiot was going to arrest the kid, I mean Miz Parkhurst, and put her in jail until he has time to figure out what happened to Raiter. Jake put a stop to that notion, but he thinks maybe you ought to hang around town for a few days just to make certain it don't happen again."

He didn't even have to ponder his answer. "I'll do that."

Case didn't step aside.

"What else does Jake want me to do?" Tal asked, pretty

sure Case wasn't acting on his own.

"Uh, the burying is gonna be private. Just the family, except the kid, she ain't going."

That was the news Tal wanted. "Where is she?"

"I don't know for sure. She was out early, to the telegraph office and the stable. Crock saw her. He said she was down there feeding that old red mule a apple. Damned if she ain't a corker."

Tal smiled.

"Likely she's at Raiter's house."

"Thanks, Larson, I'll—" Tal started to step around him.

"Uh, Jones, I ain't sure how much you can see, but I reckon I oughta tell you that I ain't sure how the kid fooled us into thinking she was a boy. I saw her myself and she makes a handsome woman. And, if it comes to mind, I wouldn't find it amiss iffen you tell her I said so."

Tal heard the admiration in Larson's voice and took the compliment in the spirit it was given. "Thanks," he said, "I'll do that."

He knew Case was standing on the boardwalk, watching him go, but he wasn't sure what else the man wanted until Larson said, "Take good care of her, Jones, and don't—"

Stopping, he turned around and asked, "Don't what?"

"Nothing. I was . . . Hell, it ain't none of my look in what happens to—"

"What are you talking about?"

"The kid's family. Her ma and the rest of them. They don't know . . . Jones, they ain't gonna make it easy for her."

"I can't do anything about her family. Dammit, Case, you know what I am and so do they. I can't offer Edwina any kind of life. I wish I could, but . . ."

Larson didn't say anything more. He just shrugged, turned his back on Tal, and walked away. He walked slowly, but he was whistling as he headed back toward the hotel.

Tal wasn't doing any whistling when he walked up to Raiter's front door and lifted his hand to knock. It wasn't Edwina who opened the door, stared at him for a long moment, and then asked, "Mr. Jones?"

"Yes, ma'am."

"I'm Lavinia Parkhurst, Edwina's mother, and you are not welcome here."

Edwina came up behind her mother, slipped around the shorter woman and smiled at Tal. "I'm glad you came, I need to—"

"Edwina, haven't you done enough to—"

"Mother, please," Edwina admonished, her voice gentle. "Livy needs your help with the girls."

"I can't leave you here with this man. Heaven alone knows what—"

Edwina stepped down onto the stoop. "Mother, Mr. Jones has come to bid me farewell, not carry me off and have his way with me."

"Edwina!" Mrs. Parkhurst cried, sounding horrified and maybe a little frightened.

"Please, Mother." When her plea had no effect, Edwina placed her hand on his arm, and said, "Tal, I—I'm sorry. I was afraid it would be like this, but I thought maybe . . ."

He had been damned sure it would be like this, too, that her family would put her through hell, and what hurt him the most was that he couldn't do anything about it. "Kid, there's no sense in fighting it. I just came to give you this." He gave her the box of writing before he said, "Good-bye, Edwina. I wish it was different, that we could—"

"So do I," she whispered, heartbreak in every tiny speck of sound. "Oh, my dearest love, so do I."

The sun was bringing glints of gold to her soft curls and

beneath the diamond-bright sparkle of her tears, Tal was sure he saw a glimpse of blue, deep, deep blue. Those small things, and the love in her voice, were all he had of her at the moment. He stood there for an eternity that lasted less than a second and swallowed hard. "I love you, Edwina, and I always will," he choked, his voice cracking.

Chapter Twenty-Three

Edwina stood on the stoop and watched Tal walk away. Her heart went with him, her heart, her soul, and maybe even the breath from her body. If it wasn't all that, why else would it hurt so much?

When he was lost to the film of tears that blinded her, she tightened her grip on the writing box. She bit her lip and went back into her sister's house. Aching with emptiness, knowing it would always be like this, Edwina stopped just inside the door. She hugged her writing box closer to her heart and looked at her mother, silently asking for a scrap of love to ease her terrible grief.

Evidently her mother read something else in her daughter's face. "What—what are you going to do?" she asked.

Her mother's rejection sent a shiver of foreboding up Edwina's spine and hinted at what her future would be like. "I'm going to write, Mother."

Mrs. Parkhurst's small white hand came up to press against the bosom of her black silk gown. Her voice quavered. "Not another one of those horrid little books? Oh, please, Edwina, don't. If you care nothing for your own immortal soul, then think of the shame you are bringing to your poor innocent family."

She tried to explain, to make her mother understand. "Mother, I have a commitment to fulfill. I gave my word to my publisher and signed my name on the contract. If I don't do it, they can sue me, maybe even put me in jail. Besides that, we are going to need the money if we are to—"

Drawing herself up to her full height, Mrs. Parkhurst proclaimed, "Edwina, Olivia has a house now, property, and several prosperous businesses. She has promised that she will provide for us."

Grief for Tal and for the family she had so clearly lost almost drowning her, Edwina asked, "You don't need me at all anymore, Mother, is that it? Or is it that you would prefer I was out of sight, so no one could see the family shame?"

Her mother licked her lips, looked down at the rug and moved away. She might be silent, but every move and every expression on her face told Edwina that her mother might still love her, but now she was both ashamed and afraid of her old-maid daughter.

With that harsh knowledge came a modicum of relief, a small glimpse of what might be a seed of hope. It was then that the bare outline of a plan wiggled its way into Edwina's brain. She examined it for flaws. After her family left for the burial, she hummed softly as she laid out her writing material, seated herself at the kitchen table, and dipped the steel nib of her pen into the bottle of ink.

"Livy, dear, I know you have your hands full trying to take care of Ambrose's businesses, but you have to do something. My nerves truly can't stand anymore of this."

"Be patient. Beneath it all, she is still our own Edwina, Auntie. She's going through a very bad time right now and doesn't realize how much she is upsetting everyone." Olivia spoke calmly, tried to soothe their distraught aunt, but Edwina, overhearing the conversation as she came out of the bedroom into the kitchen, knew it was a futile effort.

She might still be a spinster, but she was no longer the old maid to be ordered around or an unpaid servant. At the moment, she wasn't sure just what she was, but she intended finding out very shortly.

It had taken four days, but at last the manuscripts were finished, wrapped carefully, addressed to her publisher, and ready to go out on the morning stage. Her telegrams had been answered, her instructions carried out, and her wishes fulfilled—at least most of them. The marshal had absolved her of any guilt in Ambrose's killing. Edwina had only a few more things that needed doing and not one of them was going to be easy. Taking the package and her wooden writing box with her, Edwina had gone into the back bedroom where she had been given floor space for her pallet.

She was stopped at the door by voices. She was still carrying both package and box and was wearing male garments, from the battered hat on her head to the clean britches that covered her long legs. Charlie's coat was draped over her shoulders and Tal's Colt was once more belted around her waist.

She was frightened. If this didn't work, if she couldn't convince . . . Edwina shook her head. It would work. It had to. There would be no going back because the minute she stepped through the doorway, she was going to start burning her bridges.

Taking a deep breath, she pushed the curtain aside and walked out to face her sister and her aunt, and to see the hastily concealed relief in their eyes when she told them what she was planning to do.

Tal was lying in bed, trying to stay warm, and dozing maybe, but really thinking about Edwina and hoping she wasn't hurting as bad as he was. She was being treated badly by that family of hers—or so Martha Biggs, the Parkhurst women's servant, had told him. "Spoiled and selfish, every living one of them," the old woman said, scolding him, while she put drops in his eyes and then fashioned a black patch for him to wear over the worse one.

"Edwina's the only one of them with a lick of get-up-and-get, and you're a fool if you go off and leave her here with them. It won't be a month before she's running everything for them again. And will they appreciate it? No, by all that's holy, they won't. They'll just act like that's what she's supposed to do, all an old maid like her's good for."

She paused, looked at his eye again. "I reckon I've said too much already, Mr. Jones. It's time I was getting back to Mr. Larson. Now, there's a man what knows what he wants, and I expect he's gonna get it, sooner or later."

Neither knowing nor caring what it was Jake Larson wanted, Tal just grunted something in answer and thanked her for coming to tend his eyes.

"What I did," she said, "I did for Edwina. And maybe to tell you that being shot ain't all that's made you a blind fool."

Whatever she had done to him, his sight in one eye had improved considerably. Being able to see was good, but it didn't help him figure out a way to court Edwina in a proper fashion and make her his wife.

It was too dark to see anything but, despite the noisy wind huffing around the building, he was sure he heard the doorknob rattle. Rising up on one elbow, he was reaching under his pillow for his Colt when the door creaked slightly as someone eased it open, crept into the room, and closed the door with scarcely another sound.

The hammer snicked as he thumbed it back, cocking the six-gun. "That's far enough," he said, pointing the revolver in the direction of the door.

"Don't shoot."

It was a husky whisper that could only belong to one person who couldn't possibly be sneaking into his hotel room in the dark of night. Forgetting everything but her, he eased the hammer down, dropped the gun onto the bed, and was up and moving toward her almost before he had time to draw in enough breath to ask, "What is it? What's wrong?"

It was dark in the room, but his reaching hands found her within seconds, caught her shoulders, and pulled her into his embrace. Something hard and square held them apart, but he couldn't release her. She was trembling so badly he was afraid she couldn't stand up alone. That added to his fright.

"What is it, sweetheart? What's the matter?" he asked as he led her to his bed and sat on the edge with her close beside him.

"Cold," she said through chattering teeth. "Scared."

That angered him, but he fought down the anger and asked, sounding a lot calmer than he felt, "Who in the hell scared you?"

She didn't answer at once. His arm around her shoulder, his hand and his nose discovered still another mystery. She was wearing the coat the old skinner had given her, the one that smelled of mule, smoke, sweat. She was wearing britches again, too.

"Kid," he said, trying to sound stern, "what's going on? What are you doing here?"

She wanted to tell him the plan, but she couldn't. Her mouth was dry, her palms wet. Her stomach had a bad case of the quivers and her lips felt numb.

"Please, sweetheart, tell me," he said, sounding pretty much the way she was feeling.

She hesitated. New fears raced in to assail her. What if he

. . . Edwina shook her head. Tal was a man of courage, and he was stubborn. She knew he wasn't going to change his mind unless she—

He had to. Everything else was over and done. There was only this final deed, and then . . . If she ran now, she would never know what the other feeling meant. What life could be with a man who—

"Tal, nothing's wrong. I just had to find you. There's something I needed to tell you and . . ."

"Dammit, Edwina, you can't just go chasing around at night by yourself. This town is . . . Does your family know where you are?"

"They know."

"I'll get my clothes on and see you home."

"I don't have a home." She leaned over, slid her writing box and the packaged manuscripts under the edge of his bed, and turned to face him. Almost of their own accord, her hands went up and framed his face. His arm tightened a little and pulled her closer, close enough to kiss.

He didn't kiss her. He said, "What do you mean, you don't have a home? Why are you here?"

"Because wherever you go, I'm going with you. On the stage. Tomorrow." The words came out raw, not at all like she had rehearsed.

He was silent for a long moment, and then, when he finally found his voice, he refused. "No. No, I can't allow you to throw your life away. There's your family to think of and, sweetheart, I can't take care of—"

Love rushed in, grabbed her fear, and transformed it. Her hands smoothed away the frown that was gathering on his face before her cheek touched his, her lips whispered in his ear. "I wired my publisher. I know you don't think you did anything, but I know you saved my life. Anyway, the publisher agreed with me on how the reward should be divided. There's a letter of credit for five hundred dollars waiting for you at the bank in Winnemucca. It's half of the reward money for finding Lobo Chance. I gave the other half to Jake Larson to share with the miners. I thought that was only fair."

She could hear hope being born when he said, "Very fair," and then hope faded when he added, "But five hundred dollars isn't enough for us to—"

"It's enough to take us someplace warm," she said, hugging him tighter. "A place where we can find a little house and write."

"Write?" His hands moved to her shoulders, gripped them hard, held her away from him, as if he wanted to see her face, and understand what she was saying. "Write?" he asked again. "Both of us? Together?"

The warmth spread and tingled all over her body. It brought an odd languor, which made it really difficult to breathe and sent her heart into a frenzy. "Together," she said softly, trying, with no self-consciousness at all, to move closer.

The room was icy cold. He wasn't wearing much and she knew he had to be freezing because the tremors in his body were strong enough to shake the bed, but still he held her away. His voice was hoarse when he asked, almost gasping out the words, "Your family?"

There could be nothing but truth between them now. She managed to keep the bitterness out of her voice when she explained. "They're sure I'm making a mistake, or so they said, but they didn't try to change my mind. My mother and aunt are more than happy to allow Olivia to care for them now. They're going to sell the saloon and open a mercantile."

"Kid, I'm sorry. I know how much it hurts, but it's their loss." He hugged her then, pulling her close.

Gathering her courage, Edwina sighed and whispered, "You're freezing to death. Let's go to bed."

"Sweetheart, do you know what you're saying?"

"Yes," Edwina answered, and she did know, in theory, if not in practice, and was more than willing to have him bed her, right then and right there.

Tal groaned, but even if half-frozen, he made short work of her buttons, buckles, and bootlaces while he scattered burning kisses along the way.

It wasn't a dream. She was there, warm and smooth, beside him with her nude backside tucked up tight against his growing hardness. His hand was on her small breast, caressing it with loving fingers, feeling it respond, silently inviting his mouth to taste.

He turned her onto her back and looked down at her. The morning sun was bright, falling onto her like pale gold, and he saw her for the first time. Her eyes, bluer than he would have believed possible, opened and she smiled up at him. It was the smile of a woman who had been well and truly loved and wasn't at all adverse to it happening again.

"You're beautiful," he said, pushing the blankets down, exposing her body to the light. "All of you. So damned beautiful it makes me ache."

Her contented chuckle turned to a gasp of delight and growing need as his hungry mouth found her breast and plundered its sweetness. Her hands were fondling his ears, his neck, and shoulders while his eager fingers moved down her body. They explored and stroked until her heart was fluttering in her chest and her breath rasping in as quickly as his own.

Willow slim, she was silk and satin, and Tal knew, with great satisfaction, that Edwina Parkhurst was a woman. His woman, ready and waiting to be claimed. For now and always.

Epilogue

Case Larson was standing on the stoop, holding a package, when Olivia opened the door. "This came in with the freight. Jake thought you'd want it soon, Livy, because it's from the kid."

"Edwina?" Olivia felt the familiar ache at the back of her throat, the guilt and a pang of grief. "What has she sent?"

"Why don't you open it and find out?" Case asked, his tone as gentle as the smile he gave her when she stepped back and waved him into the parlor where the rest of her family was gathered.

"Olivia, what on earth is—"

"It's from Edwina, Miz Parkhurst," Case said, tugging off his hat and looking uncomfortable. "From the looks of it, she's in San Francisco."

Jean sniffed, but both Meg and Becca put aside their mending and rushed over to Olivia. Meg took the package from Case, snipped the strings with her sewing scissors, and began to undo the wrappings.

"It's something from the newspaper," she said, holding up a clipping.

"What does it say? Let me read it," Becca cried, reaching for it.

"Give it to me, Meg, I'll read it," Olivia said, aware of how excited she sounded.

Ignoring her mother's request, Meg moved closer to the lamp and began to read. "It's headed, FAMOUS PAIR WED. It says, 'The toast of San Francisco society, the writing team of Lobo Chance (Edwina Parkhurst) and Talmadge Jones were wed today in the grand ballroom of the Ingar Hotel with some three hundred adoring fans in attendance.

" 'Dressed in her wedding finery—fringed white leather floor-length skirt, a matching shirt and wearing a crown of white roses—the new Mrs. Jones read a short excerpt from their upcoming book, *Lost in the Desert*, and received a standing ovation.

" 'After a lavish champagne reception, hosted by the mayor and his wife, the happy newlyweds boarded a ship bound for the Hawaiian Islands, where they plan to bask in the warmth and begin another book, before returning home.' "

Her disapproval plain, Jean sniffed again.

"Look, Mama," Becca said, pulling something out of the packaging material. "It's a picture. Their wedding picture." She giggled and held the stiff cardboard out to her mother. "Aunt Edwina really did get married in white leather."

Olivia took it from Becca's hand and looked at the picture of her sister and brother-in-law. A smiling Edwina stood proud, her hand resting on the shoulder of her seated husband. He was dressed in black, a black patch covering one eye, his Stetson on his knee, a handlebar mustache hiding his upper lip, and his smile matching that of his bride.

Meg studied the photograph, then reached out with one finger and touched Edwina's face. "I didn't know Aunt Edwina was so beautiful," she said softly.

Olivia shook her head, wiped at the tears that filled her

228

eyes. "To my sorrow, I'm afraid I didn't, either. I guess none of us did, Meggie, except Mr. Jones." Sighing, she added, very quietly, "Maybe it takes a blind man to recognize and appreciate true beauty."